TROUT MADNESS

Being a Dissertation on the Symptoms
and Pathology of This Incurable Disease
by One of Its Victims

Robert Traver

A FIRESIDE BOOK
PUBLISHED BY SIMON & SCHUSTER INC.
NEW YORK   LONDON   TORONTO   SYDNEY   TOKYO

FIRESIDE
SIMON & SCHUSTER BUILDING
ROCKEFELLER CENTER
1230 AVENUE OF THE AMERICAS
NEW YORK, NEW YORK 10020
COPYRIGHT © 1979 BY PEREGRINE SMITH INC.
ALL RIGHTS RESERVED
INCLUDING THE RIGHT OF REPRODUCTION
IN WHOLE OR IN PART IN ANY FORM
FIRST FIRESIDE EDITION, 1989
PUBLISHED BY ARRANGEMENT WITH PEREGRINE SMITH BOOKS,
AN IMPRINT OF GIBBS M. SMITH INC.
FIRESIDE AND COLOPHON ARE REGISTERED TRADEMARKS
OF SIMON & SCHUSTER INC.
MANUFACTURED IN THE UNITED STATES OF AMERICA

3   5   7   9   10   8   6   4   2   PBK.

LIBRARY OF CONGRESS CATALOGING IN PUBLICATION DATA

TRAVER, ROBERT, DATE.
TROUT MADNESS : BEING A DISSERTATION ON THE SYMPTOMS AND PATHOLOGY
OF THIS INCURABLE DISEASE BY ONE OF ITS VICTIMS / ROBERT TRAVER.
—1ST FIRESIDE ED.
P.   CM.
REPRINT. ORIGINALLY PUBLISHED: NEW YORK : ST. MARTIN'S PRESS. 1960.
"A FIRESIDE BOOK."
1. TROUT FISHING.   2. FISHING STORIES.   I. TITLE.
SH687.T7 1989
799.1'755—DC19   88-21459
CIP

ISBN 0-671-66195-7 PBK.

CONTENTS

Preface

THERE is a lot of amiable fantasy written about trout fishing, but the truth is that few men know much if anything about the habits of trout and little more about the manner of taking them. And still fewer of these occasional wise men will spare any time from their fishing devotionals to write about it. Our knowledge of trout is like man's tenancy on this planet: precarious and tentative. In a world where men scarcely know each other, and are at pains to fight endless wars to confirm this somber fact, it is perhaps a gratuitous display of ignorance for any man to pretend extensive knowledge of the sly and secretive trout. They are dwellers on another planet. I have fished for trout since I was a boy and I admit I still know little or nothing about them. Indeed this is one of the special fascinations of pursuing them. Perhaps it is also the beginning of trout wisdom.

This book is the story of a lawyer gone wrong; of a man possessed of a fourteen-carat legal education who has gaily neglected it to follow the siren call of trout. It has been wisely observed that many lawyers are frustrated actors, but I know of one, at least, who is simply an unfrustrated fisherman. For lawyers, like all men, may be divided into two parts: those who fish and those who do not. All men who fish may in turn be divided into two parts: those who fish for trout and those who don't. Trout fishermen are a race apart; they are a dedicated crew—indolent, improvident, and quietly mad.

The true trout fisherman is like a drug addict; he dwells in a tight little dream world all his own, and the men about him, whom he observes obliviously spending their days pursuing money and power, genuinely puzzle him, as he doubtless does them. He prides himself on being an unbribed soul. So he is by way of being a philosopher, too, and sometimes he fishes not because he regards fishing as being so terribly important but because he suspects that so many of the other concerns of men are equally unimportant. Under his smiling coat of tan there often lurks a layer of melancholy and disillusion, a quiet awareness—and acceptance—of the fugitive quality of man and all his enterprises. If he must chase a will-o'-the-wisp he prefers that it be a trout. And so the fisherman fishes. It is at once an act of humility and small rebellion. And it is something more. To him his fishing is an island of reality in a world of dream and shadow. . . . Yet he is a species of unregenerate snob, too, and it pains him endlessly even to *hear* the name King Trout linked in the same breath with bass, pike, muskies, or similar representatives of what he is more likely to lump ungenerously as members of the lobster family.

All of these yarns are laid in the Upper Peninsula of Michigan, where I was born, a remote and sprawling region lying farther north than many points in Canada; a rugged land practically surrounded by the waters of two inland seas, Lake Superior and Lake Michigan. Many modest cities have larger populations than the whole U. P., a forgotten region which was virtually ignored in the westward surge of population. The canny lumber and steel barons, however, did not ignore the U. P., and they have doggedly hacked and clawed away at it for generations. Despite their best efforts, however, they still haven't quite been able to cut it down or blast it out. The brooding hills and gloomy swamps and endless waterways are still here. And the beaver. The people who inhabit the place are mostly from northern regions: Finns, Scandinavians, French-Canadians, with a generous sprinkling of the ubiquitous Irish, resourceful Cornish iron and copper miners, who were followed by the volatile Italians, and a mixed scattering of peoples from central Europe.

The simple truth is that the U. P. is one of the best hunting and fishing areas in the United States. It possesses three of nature's noblest creations: the ruffed grouse, the white-tailed deer, and the brook trout. Besides that there are sharp-tailed grouse, rabbits and black bears galore, some excellent rainbow and brown trout fishing, not to mention shoals of such tourist fish as bass, walleyes, muskies, crappies, bluegills and assorted stuff like that.

This fact, thank the Lord, is not yet widely known. It would be ironic—and a hideous thought to contemplate—if this little book should help bring about the discovery of the "forgotten" Upper Peninsula. Yet I take comfort when I reflect that the people who might find and deflower my native heath rarely hold still long enough to read books. And, I may ruefully add, they seem to have developed a special resistance to reading fishing books, like books of poetry, and somewhat like mosquitoes that finally learn to thrive on D.D.T. Apparently all that these people will willingly read are billboards, speedometers, funny books, road maps and signs proclaiming more Kozy Kabins five hundred yards ahead. They obediently race through here all summer long, sightlessly hissing along their labeled channels of concrete, bent only upon making five hundred miles a day, an achievement which somehow seems to ease the peculiar nature of their pain. They know not of the existence of the true U. P. They've never really been there.

In my view the best time to go trout fishing is when you can get away. That is virtually the only dogma you will be exposed to in this book. If you seek sage dilations on lunar tables, tidal impulses, wind phases, exotic fly patterns, tinted leaders, barometric pressures, and the like, then gently close this book and go fishing instead. Nor will you find herein any pictures of one big fish holding aloft another, the victor being identified largely by his triumphant grin. To this fisherman the fish in fishing happens to be what the onion is to onion soup: one of the main ingredients, yes, but far from everything. I fish mainly because I love the environs where trout are found: the woods; and further because I happen to dislike the environs where crowds of men are found: large cities; but if, heaven forbid, there were no trout and men were everywhere few, I would still doubtless prowl the woods and streams because it is there and only there that I really feel at home.

Successful fly fishing for trout is an act of high deceit; not only must the angler lure one of nature's subtlest and wariest creatures, he must do so with something that is false and no good—an artificial fly. Thus fake and sham lie at the heart of the enterprise. The amount of Machiavellian subtlety, guile, and sly deception that ultimately becomes wrapped up in the person of an experienced trout fisherman is faintly horrifying to contemplate. Thus fiendishly qualified for a brilliant diplomatic career he instead has time only to fish. So lesser diplomats continue to grope and bumble and their countries continue to fall into war. The only hope for it all, I am afraid, is for the Lord to drive the trout fishermen into diplomacy or else drive the diplomats to trout fishing. My guess is that either way we'd be more apt to have more peace: the fishermen-turned-diplomats would hurriedly resolve their differences on the trout stream so that they might return to their fishing, while the diplomats-turned-fishermen would shortly become so absorbed in their new passion they'd never again find time for war.

In this book I will lie a little, but not much, and I would prefer to hide my lapses under the euphemism "literary license," my excuse being that I find it difficult to inject drama into a series of fishing stories unless *somebody* occasionally gets on to a good fish. Quite frequently, you know, we fishermen don't.

ROBERT TRAVER

Trout Madness

1

The First Day

THE true fisherman approaches the first day of fishing with all the sense of wonder and awe of a child approaching Christmas. There is the same ecstatic counting of the days; the same eager and palpitant preparations; the same loving drafting of lists which are succeeded in turn by lists of lists! And then—when time seems frozen in its tracks and one is sure the magic hour will never arrive—lo, *'tis the night before fishing!* Tomorrow is the big day! Perhaps it is also the time for a little poetry, however bad . . .

> *'Twas the night before fishing*
> *When all through the house*
> *Lay Dad's scattered fishing gear*
> *As though strewn by a souse . . .*

Dad will of course have been up a dozen times during the night, prowling the midnight halls, peering out at glowering skies, creeping downstairs and pawing through mounds of duffel for the umpteenth last-minute checkup, crouching over the radio listening to the bright chatter of the all-night disk jockeys, ritualistically tapping the barometer—and perhaps even tapping his medicinal bottle of Kentucky chill-chaser. . . . It is this boyish quality of innocence, this irrepressible sense of anticipation, that makes all children and fishermen one. For after all, aren't fishermen merely permanently spellbound juveniles who have traded in Santa Claus for Izaak Walton?

Just as no Christmas can ever quite disappoint a youngster, however bleak and stormy the day, so no opening day of fishing can ever quite disappoint his grown-up brother. The day is invested with its own special magic, a magic that nothing can dispel. It is the signal for the end of the long winter hibernation, the widening of prison doors, the symbol of one of nature's greatest miracles, the annual unlocking of spring.

Since this fisherman dwells at Latitude 45 it should come as no great shock to learn that on most opening days I am obliged to draw rather heavily on this supply of magic to keep up my own drooping spirits. It is sometimes difficult to remain spellbound while mired to the hub caps in mud. *Our* big opening-day problem is twofold: to know where to find ice-free open water; and then be able to get there. During the ordeal we are sometimes driven to drink.

Our opening day is the last Saturday in April, ordinarily a disenchanting season of the year that finds most back roads badly clogged if not impassable, and a four-pound ice chisel a more promising weapon with which to probe our trout waters than a four-ounce fly rod. Our lakes and ponds are usually still ice-locked; our rivers and streams are usually in their fullest flood; and the most sensible solution is to try to remember a partially open spring-fed pond or beaver dam—and then spend a good part of the day trying to get there. Hence it is that my fishing pals and I usually take several pre-season reconnaissance trips on snowshoes. But regardless of the day, always we bravely go forth, come fire, flood, or famine—or the fulminations of relatives by marriage.

On many opening days I have had to trek into the chosen spot on snowshoes. I remember one recent spring when I stood on the foot-thick ice of a pond on my snowshoes—and took eight respectable trout on *dry* flies from a small open spring-hole less than thirty feet away, skidding them home to daddy over the ice! If you don't believe it, don't let it bother you; I'm not quite sure that I believe it myself.

Since 1936 I have kept a complete record of every fishing trip I have taken. It is amazing how I can torture myself during the winter reading over this stuff, recreating once again those magic scenes, seeing again the soft velvet glitter of trout waters, hearing once again the slow rhythmic whish of the fly lines. . . . From these records one thing emerges rather clearly: past opening days were more apt to lean to the mildly tragic than the magic. Here is the actual depressing account, omitting only the technical data on barometric pressures, water temperatures, wind direction, and the like.

1936: Snowshoed into Flopper's Pond with Clarence Lott. Pond partly open. No rises, no fish, no errors. Two flat tires on way out. "Oh, what fun it is to run . . ."

1937: Same way to same place with Mike DeFant. Reluctantly kept five wizened fryers out of low peasant pride.

1938: Slugged into Werner Creek beaver dam with mudhooks on Model A. Same fellows plus brother Leo. Caught 3 small trout and a touch of double pneumonia.

1939: Hiked into Wilson Creek beaver dams on snowshoes with Bill Gray. No rises, no takers. Bill took 6 fryers on bait. Spent balance of day coaxing the old fish car back across broken bridge. Finally did it with oats soaked generously in rum.

1940: Louie Bonetti, Nes Racine and Leo and I to O'Neil's Creek dam. A beautiful day succeeded by an even more beautiful hangover. No rises, no fish, several errors.

1941: Tom Cole and Vic Snyder and I drove out to the "Old Ruined Dams." Roads open, ponds free of ice. Fair rise. Beautiful day. Tom (6), Vic (7) and I (9), all honest fryers. All day long wedges of geese honking over like crazy, sounding remarkably like the weirdly demented yowlings of a distant pack of coyotes.

1942: Same gang plus Leo, to same place, same conditions. I kept 5 fryers. Vic filled out on bait. Had fish fry that night in camp. Lost $2.50 at rum. Tossed and turned all night.

1943: (No fish and no entry of just where I went. My, my. Must have gone straight up! Maybe no gas coupons.)

1944: South camp with usual opening gang. Bucked drifts last 2 miles. High water. Picked arbutus on south hillsides. No fish in crowd. Drowned our sorrows in mead and wore twisted garlands of arbutus in our hair.

1945: To Ted Fulsher's camp with Bill Gray and Carl Winkler. Raw, cold. Northeast wind. Didn't wet a line. Won $17.00 at poker. Slept like a log.

1946: To Frenchman's Pond with gang. Our fly lines froze in the guides. Thawed lines and drove to South Camp where Leo broke out a bottle of rare old brandy. Evidently it was *too* old; after the third round I suddenly rose and clapped my hand to my mouth—and ran outside. Guess I had better stick to the reliable brands of medium rare one-year-old cookin' whisky, the kind designed for peasants of distinction—bent on extinction.

1947: Snowshoed 5 miles with Dick Tisch in to Nurmi's Pond. Snow still 3 feet deep in woods. Got caught in bitter cold mixed rain and snow. Came down with chills and vapors and spent three days in bed with a nurse. Enervating but fun. Must try same next year. Her name was Lulu.

1948: Chopped way through the winter's bountiful supply of windfalls into O'Leary's Pond with Gipp Warner and Tom Bennett. Saw 2 wobbly young bear cubs and 17 deer. Caught 2 nice trout right off bat. Chuckled mirthlessly and twirled my waxed mustaches. Then caught in sudden hailstorm, which ended all fishing. On to Birchbark Lodge, one of those quaint Paul Bunyanish roadside tourist-traps cluttered to the eaves with stuffed owls and yawning dead bass impaled on varnished boards—and possessing the cutest iddy bitty bar, made, we were solemnly assured, out of *real logs*. Next morning, snug in my doghouse, I suspected the whisky was, too.

1949: Snowshoed into Scudder's Pond with Joe Parker. Pond partly open over bubbling springs. Fish dimpling. Stood on ice and took 8 on tiny dry flies! 'Twas a miracle. Skidded them over the ice. *Skidding at Scudder's!* by George Bellows. . . . Joe took only 1 on spinning gear, the wrong medicine.

1950: To Alger County with Marquette gang. Felt like a midget. Out of seven men I was the shortest, at six feet. A tall tale! Snow, ice and high water everywhere. Didn't wet a line. Wet whistle instead. Excursion degenerated into a pub crawl. Lost count after the 17th. Heard 8 million polkas and hillbilly laments—all miraculously sung through the left nostril. Love and despair, your spell is everywhere. . . . The inventor of the juke box is a cross between a banshee and a fiend. May he and his accomplices roast in the bottom-most pits of Hell.

1951: Slugged way through deep snow into Scudder's Pond led by proud Expedition Commander Frank Russell and his new jeep. The man *searched* for snowdrifts to charge! There is a new form of lunacy abroad in the land, the victims of which are called Jeepomaniacs. They're afraid of nothing. . . . Pond ice locked as tight as a bull's horns, as the saying doesn't go. Al Paul caught 2 in outlet—trout, not bull's horns. Surprise-attacked by party of friendly natives. Entire expedition got half shot and retired in vast disorder.

Trout Madness

1952: Mud-hooked way into Frenchman's Pond with Hank Scarffe and 2 boats. Nice intermittent "business" rise. Hank and I filled out, carefully selecting our trout. Fish fat and sassy. One of the most dramatic first-day rises I ever recall. Had but 2 bottles of beer all day. La, such a fine, contrite broth of a boy. Funny thing, I become a hell of a good fisherman when the trout decide to commit suicide. This is truly a fascinating pond.

And here is a later entry:

There have been 4 hauntingly lovely days in a row, the earth smoky and fragrant with the yeast of spring, the sky cut by the curling lash of endless flights of honking geese. Last night the wind swung abruptly to the east and the thermometer and barometer joined hands in a suicidal nose dive. Hank Scarffe, Al Paul, and I set out in 34° weather, the rainy sleet freezing to the windshield upon landing. All plans awry, we foolishly tried to reach the Moose Creek beaver dams, but got stuck up to the radiator in the first charge of a drift. We then retreated west and pushed and slugged our way through acres of rotten snow into Frenchman's Pond, where Hank and I huddled like wet robins and watched Al and his new telescope girder vainly test the pond with worms. Then came the snow, and there were *whitecaps* on the pond! Al folded his girder and we looked at each other and shrugged and slunk silently away. No one proposed even a drink. Once home I drained the fish car radiator, took a giant slug of whisky, and leapt morosely into bed, pulling the covers over my head. There I remained until nightfall, dreaming uneasily that I was a boy again and lo, it was Christmas—and I had just found my stocking filled with coal. I awoke to hear the blizzard screaming insanely outside. *"Whee-e-e-e . . ."* I crept downstairs in my bathrobe and drew every shade in the place, lit a roaring fire in the Franklin stove, built a foot-high highball, put on a mile-long piano concerto by Delius, and settled down with a book about hunting in Africa by a guy named, of all things, John A. Hunter. There were no pictures of fish! Was charmed to learn that the pygmies of the Ituri forest cure eye infections by urinating in the bad eye. Found myself wishing that the red-eyed weather man would just sorta kinda drop in. Ho hum, only 8 more months 'til Christmas.

But enough of this dreary recital of frustration, hangover, and rue. As you may by now suspect, the first day of fishing in my bailiwick is something of a gamble. Usually it is considerably more devoted to drinking than fishing, a state of affairs against which I maintain a stern taboo when the fishing really gets under way. *Then* any drinking—usually a nightcap or two—comes only *after* the fishing is over and done. To me fly fishing is ordinarily quite difficult and stimulating enough without souping up the old motor. . . . But the first day is different; it is mostly a traditional spring get-together of congenial souls, an incidental opportunity to try out and find the bugs in one's equipment, and a chance to stretch one's legs and expand one's soul. I regret that it also frequently affords an excellent opportunity to entrench one-self early and firmly in the doghouse. Then comes the time for all middle-aged fishermen to sow their rolled oats. All of which brings on a final seizure of dubious poetry.

> *'Twas the morning after the first day*
> *When all through the house*
> *Echoed the moaning and groaning*
> *Of poor daddy—the louse!*

2

The Fish Car

S H E was born on an assembly line in Detroit in 1928. After a bitter childhood involving many harrowing misadventures, she was found and adopted by me on a rainy spring day in 1935. It was then that I discovered my beloved orphan, forlorn and neglected, weeping silently in an obscure corner of a used-car lot. I stared at her and she stared mournfully back at me, dripping tears. With us I guess it was a case of love at first sight. Appraisingly squinting an eye and stroking my chin, I kicked her once on a rear tire—lo! there was air in it—and then told the man I'd take her. (Why do all prospective purchasers of used cars invariably kick at one of the tires?) The adoption papers cost me one hundred dollars. The superintendent of the used-car orphanage signed and gave me her birth certificate. We formally shook hands, and I somehow drove her away under her own power. Pedestrians paused and stared at us. Once home

I broke a bottle of beer across her radiator and christened her "Buckshot."

She was a little two-door sedan with wire wheels and twenty-one-inch tires. (For my money she is also a mobile testimonial and the most enduring monument I know to the mechanical genius of Henry Ford. How many cars of other make and like vintage does one still encounter regularly on the road?) When I got her she not only looked like a tramp, she was a tramp. Among many other things, her lights, brakes, horn, muffler, and charger didn't work; you could throw a creel through the leaky roof; a wildcat had evidently been let loose at her upholstery; the clanking engine sounded like the cardiac thumpings of an expiring thresher; a cardboard carton appropriately advertising a deodorant took the place of the glass missing from the driver's door; her windshield was cracked and completely fogged over, like a pair of dime-store sun glasses, giving the driver a wavering surrealist vision of the occasional larger objects he was able to behold.

But her heart and mind and spirit were essentially sound, and when I was done with her she was a glittering mechanical dream, a sight to behold. By that time, too, the original price I paid for her had faded into a Scotchman's tip compared to the national debt. As for her owner, he was poor but proud, and not unlike a widowed mother who takes in washing and sacrifices all to support a lazy daughter in indolence and sloth.

Since then my rejuvenated Buckshot and I have spent some of the best years of our lives together. We have hunted and fished together, explored and prospected for uranium, and gathered berries and pine knots together; there have been baseless dark rumors that we have even got drunk together. . . . But mostly we have fished; yes, year after year, season in and season out, come hell or high water, we have fished. Her radiator is adorned with two leaping tin fish I stole from my youngest daughter.

When Buckshot became old and discreet enough to vote, a few years back, I rewarded her coming of age by letting her rest after each bird season. All winter long I let her just sit in the garage, with southern exposure. There she basks like Man O' War let out to pasture. It is a kind of partial retirement, a sort of annual winter vacation with pay, in recognition of her long years of valor under fire. Now she is pure fish car and she loves it. When fishing season rolls around she snorts and trembles and backfires like an old fire horse at the sound of the bell.

She is loyal to me and in my way I am loyal to her. Last spring I had a chance to adopt a sturdy and handsome young jeep at a bargain price. I was jubilant; now I could ford rivers and scale mountains. But when it came right down to signing the adoption papers and getting rid of faithful old Buckshot on the trade-in, I fell to mentally reviewing our misspent youth together. Shortly I got all sentimental and choked up. We two had been through so *much* together. . . . "The d-deal's off," I finally told the astounded jeep man, sniffling and patting patient ol' Buckshot on the fanny. I felt so guilty for wavering that all summer long I fed Buckshot on nothing but the best ethyl gas. All was forgiven and I now suspect that our marriage shall last till old age—or jeeps—do us part. Not only is she cheap at half the price; she's a jeep at half the price.

I don't mean to imply that our romance hasn't had its darker moments. There were times when I could have reared back and given her a swift kick in the differential. No, Buckshot, I haven't forgotten the occasions when you sulked and pouted and even broke down and forced your poor old boss man to walk back to town from hell's half acre. 'Member the time you developed that—er—sudden female complaint way up north off the Yellow Dog plains? 'Member how I had to walk nearly twenty miles before I hitched a ride?—and then had to fetch a doctor from the garage, along with one of those expensive wrecker-ambulances to tote you in? And then paid nearly a hundred bucks for your operation?

Eh? How's that, Buckshot? What's that you just now said? Oh, that if I'd lay off swiggling beer when I was guiding you and watched closer where I was driving, you wouldn't develop nearly so many of those aches and pains and sudden fainting spells? Well I declare—now that's gratitude for you. My, my . . . I'm truly surprised at you, Buckshot. And in front of perfect strangers, too!

My fish car is probably one of the most complete fish cars in the world. Perhaps she is *the* completest, but then I don't like to brag. This I do know: All I have to do is to get into her and drive away—and we can stay out fishing for a week. There is no further preparation and nothing I can forget (unless I forget Buckshot herself) because I always leave all of my treasures in her custody. When she and I shove off we are a sort of Abercrombie & Fitch on the march. Here is only a partial list of the gear we *always* carry; it's standard equipment: Four fly rods and a spinning rod, all of which ride snugly on rubber slings suspended from the inside roof; binoculars, a camera, a magnifying glass (for studying the birds and the bees and the stomach content of trout), four sizes of flashlights (from pencil size to Lindbergh Beacon), and even one of those old Stonebridge candle lanterns for emergencies; waders and hip boots and low boat boots, and of course all the usual endless fishing gear (*that* would take a page itself), complete with patching cement, ferrule cement, and all the many odds and ends; eight miles of miscellaneous sizes and lengths of rope; a complete set of detailed county maps of Michigan based upon late air photos and showing all waters and side roads; a bedroll and spare blanket; rain clothes and a complete change of woods clothes; a tarpaulin and pup tent; a Primus stove and nesting cook kit with all the many trimmings; assorted water canteens; a small portable icebox; grub for a week, mostly bottled or canned; and, last but not least, always a supply of beer and a bottle or two of whisky—*always* when I leave, that is.

In addition I carry two spare tires and some extra tubes; enough small spare parts to start a neighborhood garage; a hand-cranked tugger that could yank a Patton tank out of a mudhole, complete with assorted logging chains and snatch blocks and "come-alongs" and U-bolts and towing cables, together with an old car axle to drive in the ground and use as a towing anchor in treeless terrain. I also carry enough tools and assorted junk to build and furnish a ranch house. On the roof I carry my rubber boat and inside the car the boat gear including anchors, jointed paddles, kapok cushions, air pump, etc. Then I carry two axes, one hatchet, one head-hunting brush knife, two sizes of pruning shears for cleaning out difficult "hot spots," an all-size leather punch, two handsaws, nails and hammers, and enough pry bars and wrecking tools to convict me of intended sabotage and burglary. To keep in character for my felonies I usually tote a .38 special revolver. Then, to top it off, there is a six-volt overhead light bulb in the car that is so bright I can read the fine print on a bill of lading without my glasses.

And where does the driver sit? one may sensibly ask. Incredibly enough, I somehow manage to keep *both* front seats free for driver and passenger. Of course with this mound of equipment piled behind us we are usually obliged to converse in guarded whispers, lest our voices jar loose the poised glacier and bury us in the avalanche. Indeed, sometimes I have even managed to squeeze an adventurous small fisherman in the *back* seat, stashing the stuff around him, though I always thoughtfully furnish him a breathing pipe so that he does not perish on the way. "Fisherman drowned in tidal wave of fishing equipment!" is one headline we seek to avoid.

As I read over this modest inventory I am struck by the number of items I have left out. I haven't even hinted about the assorted barometers, thermometers, and depthometers, the toilet, gaming and first-aid kits, the fishtail propellers, transistor radios, and folding camp stools; nor yet about the red flares and collapsible canvas pails, the crow calls, Audubon birdcalls and Indian love calls—not to mention the aluminum waterscope I use leeringly to watch mermaids. And when my pals and I really go on a prolonged expedition and take along the trailer and all *three* of my boats, that is something to behold. Then I pile most of the gear in the flat-bottomed trailer boat, and lash the third boat on top. *Ship ahoy!* Admiral Dewey is about to steam into Manila harbor.

Last summer as I was about to shove off on big safari, Grace came out on the back porch to see me off. She studied the caravan rather thoughtfully for quite a while. She spoke slowly.

"You look," she said quietly, "you look like the addled commander of a one-man army about to launch a rocket invasion of Mars."

"Nope," I corrected her. "I'm the Ringling Brothers on my way to merge with Barnum & Bailey. Good day, Madam. Giddap, Buckshot!"

3

Big Secret Trout

No MISANTHROPIST, I must nevertheless confess that I like and frequently prefer to fish alone. Of course in a sense all dedicated fishermen must fish alone; the pursuit is essentially a solitary one; but sometimes I not only like to fish out of actual sight and sound of my fellow addicts, but alone too in the relaxing sense that I need not consider the convenience or foibles or state of hangover of my companions, nor subconsciously compete with them (smarting just a little over their success or gloating just a little over mine), nor, more selfishly, feel any guilty compulsion to smile falsely and yield them a favorite piece of water.

There is a certain remote stretch of river on the Middle Escanaba that I love to fish by myself; the place seems made for wonder and solitude. This enchanted stretch lies near an old deer-hunting camp of my father's. A cold feeder stream—"The Spawnshop," my father called it—runs through the ancient beaver meadows below the camp. After much gravelly winding and circling and gurgling over tiny beaver dams the creek gaily joins the big river a mile or so east of the camp. Not unnaturally, in warm weather this junction is a favorite convention spot for brook trout.

One may drive to the camp in an old car or a jeep but, after that, elementary democracy sets in; all fishermen alike must walk down to the big river—*even* the arrogant new jeepocracy. Since my father died the old ridge trail has become overgrown and faint and wonderfully clogged with windfalls. I leave it that way. Between us the deer and I manage to keep it from disappearing altogether. Since this trail is by far the easiest and closest approach to my secret spot, needless to say few, secretive, and great of heart are the fishermen I ever take over it.

I like to park my old fish car by the camp perhaps an hour or so before sundown. Generally I enter the neglected old camp to look around and, over a devotional beer, sit and brood a little over the dear dead days of yesteryear, or perhaps morosely review the progressive decay of calendar art collected there during forty-odd years. And always I am amazed that the scampering field mice haven't carried the musty old place away, calendars and all. . . . Traveling light, I pack my waders and fishing gear—with perhaps a can or two of beer to stave off pellagra—and set off. I craftily avoid using the old trail at first (thus leaving no clue), charging instead into the thickest woods, using my rod case as a wand to part the nodding ferns for hidden windfalls. Then veering right and picking up the trail, I am at last on the way to the fabulous spot where my father and I used to derrick out so many trout when I was a boy.

Padding swiftly along the old trail—over windfalls, under others—I sometimes recapture the fantasies of my boyhood:

once again, perhaps, I am a lithe young Indian brave—the seventh son of Chief Booze-in-the-Face, a modest lad who can wheel and shoot the eye out of a woodchuck at seventy paces—now bound riverward to capture a great copper-hued trout for a demure copper-hued maiden; or again, and more sensibly, I am returning from the river simply to capture the copper-hued maiden herself. But copper fish or Indian maid, there is fantasy in the air; the earth is young again; all remains unchanged: there is still the occasional porcupine waddling away, bristling and ridiculous; still the startling whir of a partridge; still the sudden blowing and thumping retreat of a surprised deer. I pause and listen stealthily. The distant blowing grows fainter and fainter, "*whew*" and again "*whew*," like wind grieving in the pines.

By and by the middle-aged fisherman, still gripped by his fantasies, reaches the outlet of the creek into the main river. Hm . . . no fish are rising. He stoops to stash a spare can of beer in the icy gravel, scattering the little troutlings. Then, red-faced and panting, he lurches up river through the brambles to the old deer crossing at the gravel ford. Another unseen deer blows and stamps—this time across the river. "*Whew*," the fisherman answers, mopping his forehead on his sleeve, easing off the packsack, squatting there batting mosquitoes and sipping his beer and watching the endless marvel of the unwinding river. The sun is low, most of the water is wrapped in shadow, a pregnant stillness prevails. Lo, the smaller fish are beginning to rise. Ah, there's a good one working! Still watching, he gropes in the bunch grass for his rod case. All fantasies are now forgotten.

Just above this shallow gravel ford there is a wide, slick, still-running and hopelessly unwadable expanse of deep water—a small lake within the river. I have never seen a spot quite like it. On my side of this pool there is a steep-sloping sandy bank surmounted by a jungle of tag alders. On the far opposite bank there is an abrupt, rocky, root-lined ledge lined with clumps of out-curving birches, rising so tall, their quivering small leaves glittering in the dying sun like a million tinkling tambourines. But another good fish rises, so to hell with the tambourines. . . . For in this mysterious pool dwell some of the biggest brown trout I know. This is my secret spot. Fiendishly evasive, these trout are not only hard to catch but, because of their habitat, equally hard to fish. The fisherman's trouble is double.

A boat or canoe invariably invokes mutiny and puts them down—at least any vessel captained by me. My most extravagant power casts from the ford below usually do the same or else fall short, though not always. The tall fly-catching tag alders on my side discourage any normal bank approach consistent with retaining one's sanity. (Hacking down the tag alders would not only be a chore, but would at once spoil the natural beauty of the place and erect a billboard proclaiming: BIG TROUT RESIDE HERE!) Across the way the steep rocky bank and the clusters of birches and tangled small stuff make it impossible properly to present a fly or to handle a decent trout if one could. The place is a fisherman's challenge and a fisherman's dream: lovely, enchanted, and endlessly tantalizing. I love it.

Across from me, closer to the other side and nicely out of range, there is a slow whirl-around of silky black water, endlessly revolving. Nearly everything floating into the pool —including most natural flies—takes at least one free ride around this lazy merry-go-round. For many insects it is frequently the last ride, for it is here that the fat tribal chieftains among the brown trout foregather at dusk to roll and cavort. Many a happy hour have I spent fruitlessly stalking these wise old trout. The elements willing, occasionally I even outwit one. Once last summer I outwitted two—all in the same ecstatic evening. Only now can I venture coherently to speak of it.

I had stashed my beer in the creek mouth as usual and had puffed my way through the tangle up to the deep pool. There they were feeding in the merry-go-round, *both* of them, working as only big trout can work—swiftly, silently, accurately—making genteel little pneumatic sounds, like a pair of rival dowagers sipping their cups of tea. I commanded myself to sit down and open my shaking can of beer. Above and below the pool as far as I could see the smaller brook trout were flashily feeding, but tonight the entire pool belonged to these two quietly ravenous pirates. "Slp, slp" continued the pair as I sat there ruefully wondering what a Hewitt or LaBranche or Bergman would do.

"They'd probably rig up and go fishin'," at length I sensibly told myself in an awed stage whisper. So I arose and with furious nonchalance rigged up, slowly, carefully, ignoring the trout as though time were a dime and there were no fish rising in the whole river, dressing the line just so, scrubbing out the fine twelve-foot leader with my bar of mechanic's soap. I even managed to whistle a tuneless obbligato to the steady "Slp, slp, slp. . . ."

And now the fly. I hadn't the faintest idea what fly to use as it was too shadowy and far away to even guess what they were taking. Suddenly I had *the* idea: I had just visited the parlor of Peterson, one of my favorite fly tiers, and had persuaded him to tie up a dozen exquisitely small palmer-tied creations on stiff gray hackle. I had got them for buoyancy to roll-cast on a certain difficult wooded pond. Why not try one here? Yet how on earth would I present it?

Most fishermen, including this one, cling to their pet stupidities as they would to a battered briar or an old jacket; and their dogged persistence in wrong methods and general wrongheadedness finally wins them a sort of grudging admiration, if not many trout. Ordinarily I would have put these fish down, using my usual approach, in about two casts of a squirrel's tail. Perhaps the sheer hopelessness of the situation gave me the wit to solve it. Next time I'll doubtless try to cast an anvil out to stun them. "The *only* controlled cast I can possibly make here," I muttered, hoarse with inspiration, "is a *roll* cast . . . yes—it's that or nothing, Johnny me bye." If it is in such hours that greatness is born, then this was my finest hour.

Anyone who has ever tried successfully to roll-cast a dry fly under any circumstances, let alone cross-stream in a wide river with conflicting currents and before two big dining trout, knows that baby sitting for colicky triplets is much easier. For those who know not the roll cast, I shall simply say that it is a heaven-born cast made as though throwing an overhand half-hitch with a rope tied to a stick, no backcast being involved. But a roll cast would pull my fly under; a decent back cast was impossible; yet I had to present a floating fly. *That* was my little problem.

"Slp, slp, slp," went the trout, oblivious to the turmoil within me.

Standing on the dry bank in my moccasins I calmly stripped out line and kept rolling it upstream and inshore— so as not to disturb my quarry—until I figured my fly was out perhaps ten feet more than the distance between me and the steadily feeding trout. And that was plenty far. On each test cast the noble little gray hackle quickly appeared and rode beautifully. "God bless Peterson," I murmured. Then I began boldly to arc the cast out into the main river, gauging for distance, and then—suddenly—I drew in my breath and drew up my slack and rolled out the fatal business cast. *This was it.* The fly lit not fifteen feet upstream from the top fish—right in the down whirl of the merry-go-round. The little gray hackle bobbed up, circled a trifle uncertainly and then began slowly to float downstream like a little major. The fish gods had smiled. Exultant, I mentally reordered three dozen precious little gray hackles. Twelve feet, ten feet, eight . . . holding my breath, I also offered up a tiny prayer to the roll cast. "Slp, slp . . ." The count-down continued—five feet, two feet, one foot, "slp"—and he was on.

Like many big browns, this one made one gorgeous dripping leap and bore down in a power dive, way deep, dogging this way and that like a bulldog shaking a terrier. Keeping light pressure, I coaxed rather than forced him out of the merry-go-round. Once out I let him conduct the little gray hackle on a subterranean tour and then—and then—I saw and heard his companion resume his greedy rise, "Slp, slp." *That* nearly unstrung me; as though one's fishing companion had yawned and casually opened and drunk a bottle of beer while one was sinking for the third time.

Like a harried dime-store manager with the place full of reaching juvenile delinquents, I kept trying to tend to business and avoid trouble and watch the sawing leader and the other feeding trout all at the same time. Then my trout began to sulk and bore, way deep, and the taut leader began to vibrate and whine like the plucked string of a harp. What if he snags a deadhead? I fretted. Just then a whirring half-dozen local ducks rushed upstream in oiled flight, banking away when they saw this strange tableau, a queer man standing there holding a straining hoop. Finally worried, I tried a little more pressure, gently pumping, and he came up in a sudden rush and rolled on his side at my feet like a length of cordwood. Then he saw his tormentor and was down and away again.

The nighthawks had descended to join the bats before I had him folded and dripping in the net, stone dead. "Holy old Mackinaw!" I said, numb-wristed and weak with conquest. A noisy whippoorwill announced dusk. I blew on my matted gray hackle and, without changing flies, on the next business cast I was on to his partner—the senior partner, it developed—which I played far into the night, the nighthawks and bats wheeling all about me. Two days later all three of us appeared in the local paper; on the front page, mind you. I was the one in the middle, the short one with the fatuous grin.

Next season I rather think I'll visit my secret place once or twice.

4

Green Pastures

FISHERMEN are a perverse and restless lot, constantly poised to migrate to greener pastures, ever helpless recruits for the wild-goose chase. They're apt to be up and away at the drop of an idle rumor. Indeed this willingness to pursue the will-o'-the-wisp of the true trout fairyland, this curious readiness to chase bubbles, mirages, and rainbows up and down the land, seems to make up half the lure of fishing. Some wild-eyed mosquito-crazed character sidles up to another fisherman and furtively mumbles, "I just heard of a place where they splash waves in your face"—and off they zoom to the moon, gaily negotiating seven cedar swamps on the way.

Any fisherman with red fish blood in his veins has himself made these wild excursions, only to return, flushed and fishless, "when the day is far spent, smelling of strong drink, and the truth is not in him." All of us are guilty. Fishermen who no longer heed these siren calls have either become ex-fishermen or old fishermen. . . . On the other hand some of the best trout spots I have ever known were divulged to me quite by accident, and frequently were disclosed when my mind was miles—well, anyway six inches—away from thoughts of trout.

There was the historic occasion when I drove to the remote logging village of McFarland to settle a workmen's compensation accident case with a game-legged tobacco-chewing fellow who'd injured his knee. Inasmuch as I was a fishing stranger in those distant parts, it looked as if any serious fishing was shot for the day. And on the way there I hadn't even crossed a decent creek. Certainly all this was a dubious prelude to the discovery of some of the most fabulous brook trout fishing I have ever encountered. My man signed the release papers, I gave him his check, and he spat. Thus unpouted, he managed to thank me and then tried to pay me some money for my trouble. Pushing Satan behind me, I thanked him and virtuously explained that my fee was being paid by the other side, by whom I was retained. My grateful chum still insisted.

"Here, take ten bucks, anyway." He squinted discerningly. "Go buy yourself a coupla drinks—you kinda look like you could stand a few snorts."

"Look, friend," I said, mostly to avoid offending the gracious little man, and so that I might get going, "if you still insist on doing something nice for me, suppose some day when your leg gets better you take me out and show me a good trout spot in your bailiwick." It was one of those defensive and purposely vague fishing dates fishermen are always making and rarely keeping.

But my man was a pragmatist; efficient, purposeful, and a bear for action. "Hell, Mister," he said in an Is-that-all-you-want tone of voice, "I'll take you *now!* Got your fishin' tackle along?"

"I always carry it—even to weddings," I announced truthfully. (My wife still bitterly suspects that I smuggled my fishing gear along on our honeymoon. Otherwise, where had I disappeared to, hours on end? The truth is that it was just some darned old fishing equipment I had meant to give away to some junior anglers and had instead forgotten and left in the back of the car. . . .)

"Come with me," he said, and I, putty in his hands, followed directions obediently. "An' don't you worry none about my leg," he added, winking. "I got my money, ain't I?"

After not more than thirty minutes of driving over a serpentine maze of dirt side roads my new chum stopped me at a dubious-looking foot-wide rivulet running through a galvanized-iron culvert, and then—his extravagant compensation limp now miraculously cured—plunged me upstream through a tangle of assorted brambles into a little jewel of a beaver dam—high and narrow, deep and black as India ink, crisscrossed with fallen cedars, and backed up as far as the eye could see.

"This is it," he said, wrenching apart the joints of a steel girder he was carrying—known in some quarters as a telescope pole—and threading a half-dozen of what he engagingly called "pork chops" (night crawlers to me) on to a bait hook the size and hue of half of a rusty ice tongs. This done he stomped up to the dam and, whirling the loose coils of line 'round and 'round him as though he were about to rope a bronco, finally lofted this fantastic blob of writhing bait out across the dam. It landed with the genteel plop of an anvil dropped from an airplane. "He must be aiming to *stun* them," I thought, shutting my eyes in quiet horror—

and opening them only to find him disengaging a plump twelve-inch brook trout from his harpoon.

"N-nice one," I ventured.

He spat an amber stream of Peerless juice that must have raised the dam six inches, looked up at the sky, shook his head, and spoke. "Nope, guess the big ones ain't hittin' yet. Too bright'n early."

He and his portable crane had miraculously horsed out five more nice trout before I was fairly rigged up, and then he stomped away and disappeared around a bend upstream. I teetered out onto the middle of the beaver dam, my hands shaking a little as I selected and tied on a small red and white candy-striped hair fly tied by Paul Young. If my chum could do *that* with worms and that steel beam he'd stolen from the Brooklyn Bridge . . .

"Here goes," I murmured, flipping her out on a preliminary non-business cast, not more than fifteen feet.

An ascending *cone* of trout rushed up and literally fought for the fly. It was by all odds the damndest thing of its kind I ever saw. In my delirium I nearly keeled back off the dam. The problem was not to get on to a trout; the *big* trick would have been to successfully snatch the fly away before one of them grabbed it. I stood there in the middle of the dam in a blazing sun and calmly—perhaps not so calmly—filled out, keeping nothing under ten inches and returning but two. And they were all plump, dark-backed native beauties with flaming flanks. All told it couldn't have taken a half-hour. They ran up to thirteen inches; not fabulous, I agree, but nice brook trout in any fisherman's league. I hadn't had fishing quite like it since I was a kid.

My chum and his girder finally clanked around the bend. His limp had totally disappeared and I reflected on the re-markable therapeutic properties of that faithful old miracle drug: *money*. He found me sitting on a cedar log, smoking and watching the first trout beginning to roll, my own trout cleaned and neatly laid away in my creel, my rod taken down. He spat—"Plink!"—and spoke.

"What luck?" he chirped.

"Good," I chirped back, grinning smugly.

"How many?"

"Fifteen," I answered proudly.

"Hm. . . . Aintcha gonna ketch your limit?" he said, frowning.

"Whatcha mean, *limit*?" I said.

"Why, thirty," he said, "I only got twenty-seven. They ain't hittin' jest right today."

I sagged on the log but remained conscious. "Look, chum," I said, rallying a little. "Look, the present limit for one day is *fifteen*. Didn't you know? The legislature changed it recently—just about twenty-five years ago."

My new friend stood looking at me in amazement, chewing ruminantly and wagging his head incredulously. Then he spat a new stream that I feared would surely wash out the dam. "Well, whadya know, now whadya know," he murmured, completely baffled by all the newfangled legislative innovations seeping north out of Lansing. (The limit *now* is ten.)

For several years this beaver dam presented such wonderful but essentially rather boring fishing (it was so easy), that I christened the place "The Icebox." Never once did it fail, a rare phenomenon in the present crowded world of trout fishing. Then one spring I went there to find the main dam freshly blasted out, quite evidently the work of an illegal beaver trapper. All I could catch in the trickling ruined waters was an endless parade of wriggling chubs. I nearly wept with sorrow and rage that such a natural trout habitat should have been ruined to provide a fur coat for some silky blonde on Fifth Avenue. I've never been back, though I know I should return on the long chance that a new generation of beaver may also have returned—and in the further hope that the villainous trapper either tripped and snapped his whizzle string or else died or got religion.

Ah, yes, green pastures! One Saturday afternoon in a smoky bar, where I had gone to have a quick beer while my fish car was being gassed up, an amiable Finnish pulp cutter weaved uncertainly up to me and plucked at my sleeve and said, "Yonny, you the lawyer bucko who so crazy for fish, yes? You da fella what like for fish trouts, yes? You like me show you fine place for ketch big trouts, yes?"

"Yes," I confessed to the entire indictment as I tried to quell the familiar surge of juvenile excitement over the visions of a new fishing spot. "Here we go again," I thought, recognizing all the fatal symptoms. "W-when do we leave, Toivo?" I said, surrendering unconditionally.

Two hours and some thirty miles later Toivo and I jolted to a stop on a little sand hill overlooking a vast cranberry bog in the center of which a large crescent-shaped lake lay glittering in the late afternoon sun.

"Dis here is Loon Lake," Toivo said, yawning and curling up in the car to nurse the remnants of his pint bottle while I leapt out to conduct the assault. The next four hours I spent in leaping and bouncing around on the bedspring cranberry bog, like a trapeze performer on his safety net. I flung flies, spinning lures, flatfish and spoons—I would doubtless have hurled out knives and forks had I had them—until my arm ached. Not only were there no takers, but I saw nary a sign of a fish during the entire siege. A snoring Toivo roused himself when I dragged myself back to the car.

"How many?" he grunted, blinking.

"No luck," I grunted back.

"No *luck*?" he said, astounded.

"No luck, Toivo," I repeated patiently, putting the place down as just another of those wild-goose chases. I felt one small comfort; at least there would be one less goose to chase that season. Inevitably each year there seems to be a certain number.

"What kind vorms you using?" he inquired.

"I never use worms," I replied, drawing myself up haughtily. I charitably concluded that Toivo was unaware that fishermen have become involved in duels for insinuating less.

"Oh, but you gotta use vorms," Toivo said, shaking his head over such perverse stupidity. "Dose big yuicy night crawlers—he vork da best."

I was glum and preoccupied as I unrigged. It was nearly dark as I nosed the throbbing Model-A around to take off. I silently wished for a plague to visit this malarial spot.

"*Look!*" Toivo said, pointing back at the lake.

I looked and in the gathering gloom I saw that the whole vast lake had suddenly come to a boil; it was alive with leaping and mighty rises. The fish were huge and there must have been scores and hundreds of them. It was fierce, spectacular, unbelievable. *Never* have I seen a trout rise to equal it, anywhere, and I have fished for years in Canada as well as here. . . .

"Toivo," I said, my voice grown beseeching. "C-can you wait till I rig up and t-try her again?"

Toivo shook his head. "No siree, Yonny, I can't vait no any longer. I'm late now, already. I got date my missus over vun hour ago. My missus she's big fat crabby an' if I vait nudder minoot I guess I better build camp an' stay."

If Toivo had been just a trifle less potted I would have cheerfully given him the fish car and walked back. Anything to stay. But he was too far gone for me to entrust my beloved old Buckshot to his uncertain care.

"I see, Toivo," I said, for I dolefully saw. So I cast one last wistful farewell look at the miracle rise and drove sadly away. I've never been quite the same man since. I am charmed to report that Toivo's "big fat crabby" wife wasn't even ready when I finally delivered him and the remains of his bottle up to her tender mercies.

"Wat da hell you come home so soon for?" was the shrill opening shell she fired in her bombardment.

After that I virtually moved my law office out to Loon Lake. I haunted it by day and by night. I ranged the bouncy shore like a crazed water buffalo, flinging flies and guttural oaths, but nary a pass or a strike—*and never did I see another solitary rise!* Then one evening I fetched my old bait-fishing friend, Louie Bonetti, elaborately swore him to secrecy, and sat him down on an old beer case and took off on my usual lunges. When I had made the course and returned he was in the act of derricking out a beauty with his pork chops. He had several more like it folded away in his big creel, the tails protruding. Toivo was right; worms were the medicine.

"Gooda place, Yon," beaming Louie said, grinning his million-dollar grin. "You lak borrow some pork chop?" he teased.

I then switched despondently to deep-running spinning lures and finally managed to dredge up several trout up to fourteen inches—juveniles compared with the whoppers I had seen that first enchanted evening. And anyway I wanted perversely to take them on flies. The thing had become an obsession. The truth was that Loon Lake was fast driving me loony.

Some anglers I know can't quite decide just what kind of green pastures are the most wearing on fishermen: those in the great majority that turn into wild-goose chases; those rarer ones that sometimes actually deliver; or those rarest ones of all, like Loon Lake, that are simply crawling with magazine-cover trout, and steadily defy one's best efforts to take them on flies.

As one angler this I do know. It was bad enough to find and lose that heavenly little "icebox" beaver dam, the one that became ruined, but offhand I am aware of no fishing torture quite like a fisherman *knowing* of a lake full of gorgeous trout, and not being able to so much as *lose* a fly to a single one of them! Sometimes in the middle of those warm summer nights, when the subdued crickets are quietly ticking and humming and a brooding sense of mystery pervades the air, I wake up with sudden cold sweats and lie there and think: Now, here, tonight—at this very moment— that lovely baffling lake is probably boiling with giant trout rises—and here I am, writhing in my moist bed of frustration. About then I shuffle down the hall and tilt the aspirin bottle.

I finally had to quit going to Loon Lake. I had to quit it in order to maintain three things: my wavering sanity, the remnants of my law practice, and that state of uneasy truce known as marriage. I'll venture there again only under one circumstance: Merely to guide some courageous fisherman who'll first promise under oath to use nothing but flies—and who honestly thinks he knows of a way to raise them on flies. The line of applicants will please form on the left.

As for me, when that happens I think I'll just curl up in

the fish car with my bottle, and when the first crazed volunteer bounces back to the firm ground of reality I'll hand out the bottle and leer red-eyed at him and say: "See! Didn't I tell you? It's just like Toivo said: Dose big yuicy night crawlers—he vork da best!"

5

Sinning Against Spinning

"THIS is the place, Frank," I said, ducking through the last wedge of intervening cedars.

It was a still summer evening and the sun was slowly curving down to bed. Frank Russell and I stood at last on the soggy, bedspring bank of a remote little jewel of a trout pond. A ragged unbroken wall of tall cedars literally pressed at our backs.

"See that nice trout feeding out there, Frank?" I said, pointing pondward some hundred feet.

"Barely," Frank answered cynically, shielding his eyes Indian fashion and peering through a dancing fog of delighted mosquitoes.

"Want to see me ketch 'im?" I bragged softly, ignoring both Frank's sarcasm and the feasting mosquitoes.

"I *dare* you to," Frank answered, glancing dubiously over his shoulder at the looming cedars. "But just how do you propose to drop a lure out there—by slingshot, balloon, or helicopter?"

"Watch!" I said with insufferable superiority, and I quickly assembled my magic new glass spinning rod, threaded on the hair-like monofilament nylon line, tied on a plastic casting bubble and a bare fly hook, impaled a live grasshopper on the hook, and triumphantly croaked, "Here goes!"

With one casual flip I cast the lure; it arched out truly over the rise—"plop"—; and I barely straightened out the spider-web line when the fish whammed it—and we were on to our first trout, and a nice one, too.

"Well, I'm a bowlegged tadpole!" Frank said, awestruck. "So *that's* what you call spinning?"

"Yup," I said, proudly reeling in and grinning fanatically. "Yup, this is the new love of my life."

This deathless drama unfolded some eight or ten years ago. As I recollect Frank and I each took several fair trout that evening, mostly on live grasshoppers and one or two on artificial flies. We missed at least twice as many strikes because of the inevitable slack and stretch in the spinning line—one of the smaller headaches in spinning—but despite all this Frank became an immediate and burning convert to spinning.

"Order me one of those outfits, Johnny!" he said as we ducked and threaded our way back to the fish car. "Do it *tomorrow!*"

"Your most idle whim is a command, sir," I said. "But how about our having a soothing beer to celebrate your initiation into the dark mysteries of spinning?"

As we rattled back to town, flushing the crouching nighthawks off the dirt road like mad, Frank sat in silence. Finally he spoke.

"You know, Johnny," he said. "These casting bubbles are

all right—novel as hell—but this spinning business would *really* be something if they could find a way to cast a lure—say a number eighteen dry fly—and have the casting weight fall off once the fly was floating 'way out there. That way there'd be no clumsy and distracting plastic float either to scare the fish upon landing or on the retrieve or to slow the strike when the fish hits."

Frank was catching on fast. "Smart boy," I said. "You've divined one of the main headaches of this form of spinning in one easy lesson. There's only one small hitch—how're you going to do it?"

"Yes," Frank continued thoughtfully, as though talking to himself. "Yes," he repeated, "the problem is to find some sort of expendable casting weight. Hm . . . now let's see. . . ."

Two days after he got his new spinning outfit, Frank Russell solved the problem of spin-casting even the tiniest dry flies fabulous distances and then, equally important, floating them. He's that kind of a guy. He solved it by use of an ingenious expendable lead casting weight that falls off immediately upon contact with the water, leaving the fly floating high and dry. He calls his simple contraption the Russell Castaway, but I shall not explain it in more detail here because his application for a patent has not yet been granted. Instead I shall pause and dilate a little on conventional spinning itself.

As everyone who has ever held a fish pole now knows, spinning (known as "threadlining" in England) is a fairly new method of sport fishing imported from Europe, the chief feature of which revolves about a free-stripping, fixed-spool, anti-backlash reel. A fine line, of leader thickness, is usually employed along with some sort of weight—whether in the lure or otherwise—to strip the line off the reel when the cast is made. For in spinning, unlike in fly-fishing, it is not the *line* that is cast but the *lure*. To this extent it is more nearly like bait-casting.

The practical advantages of spinning are manifold: even a child can cast a lure incredible distances; cautious big fish are thus more easily approached and more frequently caught off guard; little or no casting room is necessary for the out pitch; clumsy Mortimer Snerd himself couldn't foul the line; and normally unreachable water can thus be covered with deception and ease.

Back in the dear dead days of B. S. (before spinning), the line drums on all bait-casting reels revolved as the line was unwound with the cast, as though one were stripping off thread from a revolving spool held on a nail, much like the old Halloween rat-a-tats kids once used on the neighbors' windows. Frequently, however, the unwinding reel ran faster than the outgoing line, particularly near the end of the cast, creating that fisherman's horror known as the backlash. Every season I still run across an occasional fisherman sitting quietly on some remote bank, mumbling in his beard, still trying to unsnarl his casting line. "How's it coming, pal?" I usually whisper and quietly pass on. They never even look up. . . .

Then along came the revolutionary spinning reel with its stationary line-storage drum—and gone was that particular form of fishing madness. For in spinning, the line-storage drum (or spool) remains stationary as the line (or thread) is drawn off over the stationary *end*, not the revolving *side*, of the spool. There can be no backlash because the line merely dribbles off the end of the spool and, whether cast fast or slow, there is no possible way it can get snarled in the reel. Take an ordinary spool of thread and try it yourself.

The consequent decrease in casting resistance and lowered friction coupled with the general ease in casting thereby permits a child—and even ladies in slacks—to cast fabulous distances. Many of my old fly-fishing friends took up this comparatively new sport and some have become wedded to it to the virtual exclusion of their fly fishing. I became wedded, too, but I have since gotten a divorce and I'll tell you why.

With my customary childish curiosity and helpless compulsion to possess every new fishing gadget that comes along, I too fell for spinning—hook, line, and sinker. Some two-hundred-dollars-worth-of-equipment later I woke up, rubbed my eyes, and decided that I did not give a tinker's damn for this new method of taking trout. In fact I gave up spinning before many fishermen in these parts had even heard of it, and instead returned to my fly fishing with, if possible, an even greater sense of joy and dedication.

I admit everything that the increasingly numerous slaves to spinning claim for their new sport; and I recognize much of its charm and fascination. It is not so much that I hate spinning, but rather that I love fly fishing so much better. For one thing I happen to prefer to strike and play my fish on or near the surface, and typical spinning is generally done with deep-running lures for the reason that the conventional spinning lure *also* is the casting weight that is necessary to strip out the line. I have also long been familiar with and have used the various hookups of the floating plastic bubble (and similar devices) with a wet or dry fly, but I somehow do not like either casting or fishing with them. This Rube Goldberg business of using tiny swivels and bubbles and all leaves me cold.

Perhaps it is largely an hitherto unsuspected sense of neatness and fitness on my part, coupled with my delight in the beauty and subtlety inherent in being part of a good cast with a fly rod, for one thing is certain: there is no doubt that these spinning get-ups can and do take fish that often cannot even be *reached* in any other way. Perhaps the dismaying sense of fishing with "hardware" offends me. Certainly I have had advantages few "spinners" possess, what with the free use of and part ownership in the fabulous but undeveloped Russell Castaway. I dunno, maybe I'm just a cream puff.

At any rate, another serious drawback to all methods of spinning, in my book, is the comparative length of time involved in making the retrieve. Perhaps a spinning reel with an automatic retrieve might partially answer this objection, but as things stand it gets my cork to paste out a beautiful hundred-foot spinning cast and then, while reeling in, stand there and helplessly watch a nice trout rising a mere fifty feet out there or over here or over there, and not be able to immediately paste one over him. Then, more often than not, by the time I have reeled in to cast at this last rise, the fish has either moved on or else when I cast at the spot he or another fish rises a few feet to one side or the other and fingers his nose at me—while there I am 'way out there again, grating my bridgework and reeling in like mad.

The point is that any competent fly fisherman can retrieve his fly and cast it out over a rising fish—assuming it is in casting range—much quicker than can his spinning brothers. Perhaps my basic lack of interest in spinning springs from the fact that I am a slave to attempting dainty casts over rising trout; and that those stout fellows who can stand and cast out and reel in, then cast out and reel in, stolidly raking non-rising water for hour after hour, arouse my respect for their dogged patience but not any desire to copy them. I will patiently stalk rising trout by the hour, but once they sulk and go down I am inclined to join them and go pout in the car and sob over my beer until they decide to come back up to the skylight of their homes.

But none of these objections goes to the heart of the matter and I suspect that I would still prefer to fly fish for trout with the conventional split bamboo fly rod and regular tapered silk or nylon line even if all the technical objections to spinning were solved. I rather think that the simplest statement is that I find the art and ritual of fly casting a joyous and poetic experience in itself, fish or no fish. Perhaps it is sheer sentimentality or conservatism on my part; perhaps it is a stubborn desire to do things the hard way; but somehow or other I like and prefer the sense of *personal involvement* and *immediacy* and *control* that I, at least, feel only when I am delicately casting my fly over likely trout waters. By comparison I find that this thing called spinning is strictly for the birds.

There—I've finally said it! The line of dedicated and appalled spin-fishermen who wish to stone me for my heresy will please form on the left.

6

⋘⋘⋘

Lost Atlantis

I T W A S a hot lazy afternoon in mid-August.
The small fry had the radio turned on full blast, blaring out
the first game of a doubleheader between the New York
Yankees and, I guess, the Green Bay Packers. The game had
reached a pretty pass: there were two down and the bases
were loaded; some character or other from Gap Tooth, Kentucky, was coming to bat; the din was terrific. I was enchanted to learn that this man of destiny weighed 193
pounds, stood 5 feet 11, had been rejected by the draft for
night sweats, and boasted a batting average of .315. But
horror of horrors, he had popped out in the last two times
at bat. . . .

I retreated to the side porch, dark with hatred of all
organized sports in general and Sunday afternoon baseball
in particular. "Try that favorite brew of millions!" the an-
nouncer bawled after me. "Try a cool bottle of Pssst's mel-

43

low, golden, *homogenized* beer!" Ah, science had invaded even the beer vats . . . I made a mental note forever to avoid the stuff and sat staring morosely at the unkempt lawn, hot, bored, and fidgety. It was too torrid to go fishing, and anyway, I generously concluded, a responsible husband and parent owes a certain moral duty to share some of his leisure hours with his wife and children. Especially the poor kids. . . . Yes, during their formative and impressionable years a man's children need dear old dad around to—well—to sort of quietly set them an example. After all, *fishing* wasn't everything in life . . . I gave a virtuous little sniff.

Just then Grace came to the screen door and suggested that the lawn needed currying. "The place," she added acidly, "is beginning to look like an abandoned graveyard." Poor girl, she still cherishes the dream that I can ever be housebroken—at least during fishing season.

"Let's tether a goat instead and be the show place of the neighborhood," I said, ducking a withering look.

"Muskrat swings and pops up to center field!" the radio tragically proclaimed, as though announcing the fall of Rome. I squeezed my eyes shut.

Grace weighed the troubled situation. "Will you promise to mow the lawn tomorrow after work if I let you go fishing now?" she countered, trading slyly on a certain weakness she had observed in her husband.

"Madam, it's a deal," I answered brightly, already halfway out to the old fish car. With a flourish I swung open the garage doors, nearly tripped over a lurking lawn mower, and leapt into the fish car. "Giddap, Buckshot," I chortled, free as the wind, and in nothing flat I was rattling out toward Moose Creek, one of my favorite trout streams. Growing children, I mused between bounces, needed to balance their character development with the rare vitamins found only in freshly caught trout. Yes, I reflected, young ideals can best be nurtured in sturdy young bodies. Far from walking out on the kids, then, this fishing expedition, like so many others, was essentially a sacrificial labor of love.

Moose Creek is no great shakes to look at, being for the most part narrow and brushy, but the stretch where I usually hit it is a wide, shallow stream formed by an ancient inactive beaver dam which backs up the water for nearly a mile. I had been fishing there off and on for over fifteen years. The place harbors some nice brook trout but they are a temperamental lot, scary and hard to catch.

For years I had been hitting Moose Creek at this very same place—at old Camp Alice—about a half-mile upstream from the old beaver dam. I had almost always confined my fishing between the camp and the dam. While a good deal of the stretch was wadable, the margins of it were inclined to be swampy and difficult and there were also some interesting crannies and hideouts that could only be reached from a boat because of the varying depth of the water or accumulation of silt. Consequently I usually threw my rubber boat on the roof of the car whenever I planned to fish there. I had it along today.

Once or twice in recent years I had ventured upstream a little way from the usual point of embarkation, but this upper stretch was so choked and clogged with lily pads and some sort of matted and clutching water grass that I soon gave up and deeded it back to the Indians. Yup, there was no doubt about it: downstream toward the dam was by far the better place to fish. It was true that old-time fishermen used to tell me about a wonderful spring-fed beaver dam near the headwaters—"way up there in the foothills," they'd wave vaguely—but years ago, it seemed, some low genius in the conservation department had had a vision and blasted the dam out as part of some newfangled stream-improvement program. Here the old-timers would invariably choke up and dolefully wag their heads as though to say: "Mysterious are the devices of all game wardens . . ." So the word was out that the fishing upstream was all shot; and the fact was that the old fishing trails along the near bank had long since grown in and become choked with tangles of windfalls.

"Yep, yep," one old-time fisherman told me. "We'd only taken barrels of beautiful trout out of that there upper dam for nigh on to half a century—so those smart hammer-heads in the State Capitol proved the fishing was bad—so they up an' blasts her out!"

Thus it was that on a hot Sunday afternoon I reluctantly decided to go upstream and survey the historic ruins for myself. Boredom, not vision, was all that drove me to it. I leisurely wrestled the rubber boat off the fish car, gave the bladders an extra shot of air for my trip, loaded and strapped my .38 around my waist, threw my fishing gear and an old rod and a few cans of beer in my packsack, and shoved off. I paddled upstream slowly in the blazing sun, craning and listening, deliberately killing time. The voyage was on.

My first mild shock was to observe that the lily pads and thick water grass petered out before I had gotten around the second bend, the stream opening up into beautiful gravel-bottomed water in which I could see numerous small trout darting about. I had no doubt that their elders were lurking not far away. Naturally in the hot sun and the calm no fish were rising, but the spot was as trouty-looking as any stretch I had seen on the creek. "My, my," I murmured, "where has *this* place been all my life?" Of course my excuse was that I'd only been fishing the same creek for fifteen years.

I slowly pushed on and gradually the prevailing swampy shore gave way to higher land flanked in turn by low ridges, the creek narrowing and deepening, the banks now being lined with as lovely a stand of mature white pine as I had seen in many a year. Calm as it was, the soft whish and whine of the wind sifting through the tall wavy tops sounded like the muted strains of faraway violins. After another half-mile or so of this haunting vagrant music the creek narrowed down sharply.

Then I came to my first beaver dam. It wasn't much of a dam, as dams go, but the thing that quickened my pulse was the fact that it was a live dam, with fresh beaver cuttings very much in evidence. Could it possibly be? I mused, pondering what might lie above. Hm . . . let's go see.

I tossed the old rubber boat up over the dam, which didn't hold back much water, and sat perspiring in the bright sunlight sipping a can of warm beer. The big pines had now given way to a lush jungle of tag alders, the low ridges some distance away being adorned by spruces and balsams and a sprinkling of mixed second growth. I shrugged and pushed onward and upward.

In the next hour I negotiated three more fresh beaver dams, all about as modest as the first, the creek all the while getting so narrow that several times I was tempted to call it quits and head back downstream for the evening rise. But there is no lunatic quite like a trout lunatic, so each time I resisted temptation and doggedly pushed on.

Then I began to hit a series of big old white-pine wind-falls lying plump across the creek. Most annoying they were, being too low to pass under and being sufficiently high, with their scorched and jagged old branches, to give me a bad time with my boat and gear. After scaling a round dozen of these fire-scarred old giants I finally scuffed a seat for myself among the layers of bird and animal guano on the last log and sat there sweltering and had another beer and wondered what in hell I was doing way up there on a narrow miserable creek in which any decent trout would have a hard time turning around. I mopped my brow and looked at my watch and figured I could still fish the evening rise below if I abandoned this foolish enterprise and made tracks. Yes, I'd turn around and flee this malarial bog.

Just then a slight breeze came up—I swear it was a miracle—and I heard the faint but unmistakable sound of distant running water, not a trickle, not the gentle splash of a little dam, but the dull steady moan of a considerable volume of falling water. Again I squatted in the rubber boat and paddled away and in a half-hour came to a beautiful live beaver dam, at least eight feet high, from where I sat crouched in the boat below and, it seemed, at least a hundred feet long. It was a gorgeous thing.

When I had excitedly clambered up the crisscrossed beaver cuttings and finally stood on the mud-packed crest of the vast dam, trembling like a girl, I felt like Magellan or somebody beholding a new continent. The dam was loaded to the scuppers, leaking over the top in some places, and backing up a beautiful expanse of mysterious deep water as far as the eye could see. Low ridges of jack pine fringed either side. The whole thing appeared to lie in a broad ancient beaver meadow, the dry margins still being lined with old water-killed trees reaching their rigid empty branches beseechingly into the air. It was plain that untold generations of beaver had dwelt and built their dams at this spot.

From this, and the occasional weathered old workings that I saw mixed with the fresh cuttings, I was pretty sure I was standing on the same old upper beaver dam blasted

48

out years before by "those damned game wardens." The only trouble was that the oblivious beaver had ignored the fact that a dam in that place was officially *verboten*. Alas, they'd surely be arrested for violating . . . As I stood gaping, an exploring grasshopper foolishly lit on a sun-dried cutting near me. I caught and tossed him out in the dam. There was a quick swirl and a chunky trout whammed Mr. Grasshopper and flashed down and away. Hm. . . . Peering, I could see the wavering outline of a broad network of crisscrossed logs lying deep under water. The plot thickened.

Purely in the interest of science I rigged up my rod, tied on a number 12 Slim Jim—a quick-sinking wet fly—and pasted her out. *Clap!*—and I was onto a twelve-inch brook trout. Standing there in one spot on the dam in the blazing sun I took ten plucky brook trout running from ten to thirteen inches—missing twice that number—before my conscience smote me and I took down my rod. I sat and cleaned my fish, whistling while I worked, and then had my last can of beer to celebrate my new discovery. I then tossed my rubber boat over the dam, gave my bulging woven nylon creel a final loving pat, and pushed on. By then I couldn't stop and by that time, too, the sun was slacking off, and as I paddled upstream the trout were beginning to rise as far as I could see, some of them appearing larger than any I had taken or pricked. A pair of herons rose in noisy haste and flapped away in undulant flight. Ah, what a beautiful, isolated spot, I mused, delighted as a kid who had wandered into a fairy toyland.

I had not got two hundred feet above the splashing waters of my wondrous new dam before I heard something that made me nearly fall out of the boat—*the roaring rush of high-speed auto traffic!* Had mighty Magellan gone in circles and merely rediscovered Spain? I held my paddles to listen. There m-must be some mistake, I told myself, sick with dismay.

There wasn't. Another car rushed by, stridently sounding its horn. Frantic now with mingled curiosity and concern for my new dream spot, I paddled upstream in the lengthening shadows through one of the most dramatic rises of brook trout I had seen in years, the primeval calm of the spot being broken only by the ever-nearing roar and clash of car traffic and wailing horns. The combination of pristine peace and screeching mechanical din was positively weird. And in Heaven's name how, in this day and age, could there be such fabulous fishing within a stone's throw of a public speedway?

Up, up I went, like a man possessed, through perhaps a half-mile of sporty but narrowing water with lovely trout dimpling all around me. The invisible rushing cars now seemed to be practically alongside me. Pretty soon the dwarfed creek narrowed and shallowed to a rivulet so that I could no longer row. Shrugging like one of Roger's resourceful Rangers I got out and splashed upstream, dragging the boat by the anchor rope. Shortly the ridges narrowed, grown tight with jack pines, and I got into a series of shallow and intensely cold gravelly feeder springs. I then knew that I was at the headwaters of Moose Creek. But precisely where in hell was *that*?

By now it was getting dusk and I was running out of towing water, so I philosophically took my paddles apart and stashed them in my packsack, shouldered my boat, and sloshed up the dwindling main channel. All the time I could still hear the Sunday traffic rushing mildly by. A quarter of a mile of this and my creek became a mere trickle, so I veered left toward the car sounds and, with all the airy grace of a man carrying a folded double mattress, fought my pregnant rubber boat up through the thick spruce and tamarack to the jack pine on top of the ridge. There I rested and heaved and blew and mopped the sweat away and sneaked a reassuring look at my glistening trout—and longed for a beer. Then I heard the mutter of voices close by. Leaving my boat and pistol and packsack hidden in the jack pine I walked toward the voices and in no time came out into an opening—and upon a whole family of Sunday blueberry pickers, complete with picnic hampers, parked Chevrolet, and Grandma.

"Hello," I said, peering engagingly through my damp and sweat-matted locks.

The nearest picker, a kneeling, butt-sprung lady clad in revealing if scarcely becoming tight slacks, wheeled and squealed and nearly dumped her pail of berries. She stood regarding me in moist horror, as though she had seen a ghost emerge from the woods. I didn't much blame her. Another unseen car rushed by.

"Hello," I repeated. "I've been out looking for berries and I guess I got a little mixed up," I partially lied. "What road is that?" I said, motioning toward the sounds of traffic.

By this time a red-faced, perspiring man, presumably the lady's husband, quickly moved up to defend her be-slacked virtue from the hot maniac emerged from the swamp. I repeated my suave falsehood as he squinted an appraising eye at me. "The traffic you hear is on the main road between Ishpeming and Gwinn, on Highway 35," he answered warily. "You're right at the Moose Creek turn off." I blinked and shook my head at that, for I had just come over the same road on the way out fishing, and was therefore less than three miles from my car. And after all those years I was charmed to learn, for the first time, that since the dawn of man—or at least since the last glacier—my creek had always described a gigantic U. My chum kept staring skeptically at me. "What kind of berries you lookin' for in hip boots, fella?—cranberries? And what's in the bulging creel?"

Touché! I had forgotten to cache the telltale creel. I blushed prettily and piled on another whopper. "Oh, that . . . wa-water lilies! Yep, been out gathering water lilies, too . . . wife's crazy about 'em . . . got all tangled up in that awful swamp." I tittered a trifle hysterically and waved vaguely at my New Spain. "Don't ever go near it," I warned darkly. "Full of snakes and things." The lady of the slacks sidled away from me as from a crazed leper. "Look," I rattled on, swerving abruptly from water lilies and reptilian swamps, "how would you like to make yourself a fast two bucks—and have a coupla cold beers to boot?"

"Hm . . . *cold* beer? How do you mean?" he parried, devoutly rolling his eyes and moistening his lips and stroking his chin. Plainly I was now talking his language.

"For driving me over to my car on Moose Creek—at Camp Alice. What do you say?"

I think the visions of the cold beer rather than mere money turned the trick; in a half-hour I was back at the fish car and had loaded down my pal with cool foaming goodies and his cab fare and sent him on his way. As he started to drive away he leered out the window of his car, winked, and fired this parting shot: "Those are certainly the gamiest-smellin' water lilies I ever smelt, fella. If I was you I'd go clean 'em off down in the creek!"

I grinned and waved as he gunned the Chev away, and then sat down on the running board of the fish car and opened a heavenly cold beer. "A-a-ah . . ." I looked up and saw a thin slice of yellow moon. I held up the beer. "You've had a busy day, little man," I whispered. "Fish, drink, and be merry—for tomorrow we must cut the grass. *Skoal!*"

7

Back-Yard Trout Fishing

I t w a s one of those warm, soft, luminous summer evenings; the kind that commands fishermen to go forth and then makes them yearn for time to stop in its tracks. The sky was big and high and gloriously aflame, and the fanning shafts of sunlight sifting through the far-off piles of clouds looked like the very organ pipes of Heaven. I had stolen away after supper to get an hour or two of the evening rise on one of the nearby trout ponds. The old Model-A Ford and I were bumping along nicely down through the aquarium-green tunnel of an unkempt grove of second-growth maples, about three miles from my chosen pond, when—*pow!*—I had a flat, so I drew over bumpety-bump to the side of the dirt road, cursing softly as a steve-dore.

Here was a nice kettle of no fish. If I stopped to change the tire I'd have little time left over for fishing, and if I hiked it, even less. What to do? I stood looking around. Hm . . . that bald "selectively" logged hill to the left looked vaguely familiar. . . . Then I realized that I was only about a quarter of a mile from Klipple Pond, a shallow and dying old mud puddle left from the ruins of an ancient beaver dam. I hadn't fished there since I was a kid. Should I give it a visit for old time's sake? The trout fishing in it used to be very good, yes, but that was true nearly everywhere in those distant days. Then there were dark rumors, too, that the pond had been dynamited and netted in recent years; and, anyway, none of the really *good* fishermen ever fished there any more or even mentioned the place. After all, how could a fisherman in his right mind expect to catch a decent trout these days less than nine miles from town, and only *six* miles by crow flight? Perish the thought.

Thus did I consider and mentally damn old Klipple Pond. I sighed and reached for the tire irons and then paused. *Must* I spend this enchanted evening wrestling with a flat? Here I had a night out and was dying to fish (I hadn't for a whole twenty-four hours!), so I shrugged and instead dug out the necessary tackle and gear and locked the car. At least I might as well go *look* at the place. . . . In less than ten minutes I had slipped and skidded down the old needle-covered deer trail on the steep root-lined hill and was standing on the soggy and twilit-margin of the old pond. Time had not stopped in its tracks; the organ pipes had disappeared.

The old pond lay in a deep glacial bowl scooped from between abrupt wooded hills. In the closing dusk its shallow waters looked as delicately thin and blue and uninviting as dairy milk in the bottom of a porridge bowl. It was the same old pond, all right: still no bigger than a small skating rink; still dotted with myriad islands of lily pads; still with the same old grass-grown water-logged raft that had once nearly drowned me still anchored to the near shore with the same weathered upright pole. Yes, and there was still the same dying sun shaded by the mixed spruce and maple hill across from me; still the same rhythmically persistent jungle drumming of the bullfrogs—*kwonky-kunk, kwonky-kunk!*—; and still the plaintive evening calls and ghostly dartings of the same mysterious birds whose names I had never sought nor ever cared to know. . . .

I sat there reflecting that under the surface of those placid waters endless battles raged, as fierce as any wars of men. Insects fought insects; bloodsuckers fought bloodsuckers, crayfish crayfish; salamanders salamanders; and all of them warred on each other; and the trout (if still there were any) fought all of them, all the while trying to avoid the fish ducks and gulls and kingfishers, the cranes and ospreys, and all the other swift dive bombers from out of the sky. And there was always the fear of the wily and undulant otter. And then, lo, a stray man now came along and sought to ensnare the trout with cunning little deceits contrived of feathers and fur. Yes, and he too was of the same species of lordly men who still stupidly fought each other days without end. . . .

I sat there reflecting that there was something ageless and timeless about a place like this; that it couldn't have changed much since the dawn of the world; that it would probably remain much the same after restless man, whose wisdom appeared unable to keep up with his brains, finally joined hands with his fellows and soared heavenward, propelled thence by the marvels of nuclear fission. Here, at this place, was primeval solitude: the patient unfolding pattern of a sublimely indifferent nature which doubtless regarded man as no more and no less important than a gnat.

As I sat there gripped by such lofty and poetic thoughts

I heard the first splash. I crouched low and shaded my eyes against the waning sun and discerned an ever-widening wake not more than fifty feet out from me. Hm . . . Must have been a cavorting muskrat, I concluded, ready to flip my cigar pondward and flee the hungry mosquitoes. "*Plunk,*" it went again and this time—you've guessed it—I *saw* that it wasn't any mere muskrat at all, but the rise of a fine, careless, savage man-sized trout which was out after his supper and didn't give a tinker's damn who knew it.

With trembling hands I groped for my rod and clapped it together and threaded my line and tied on a leader and a pert little dry fly and teetered out a few feet in the muddy and treacherous ooze waiting for my ravenous friend to renew his challenge. All poetry and mosquitoes were forgotten.

"*Plash!*" he went again, and by this time I became blissfully aware of trout rises dimpling all over the pond. Roll-casting because of the halo of tag alders behind me, I began feeding out line to my near fish like a rodeo cowboy trying to lasso an escaping steer. Finally my stuff was out there, placed deliberately about ten feet to the right of him, so as not to put him down, and so that I might give it to him right on the nose the next time he rose—

"*P-lunk!*" he obediently rose, accepting the challenge, and I swiftly drew up the slack and rolled her like a hoop, the line rippling out like a fleeing serpent, the leader finally folding over, and the fly itself lighting upon the center of the feeding circle as gently as the wafted down of a thistle. There was a surge as my trout took it—*wham*—and I was on to him, fighting him, while all about me the frogs croaked—*kwonky-kunk*—, the birds darted and flashed and called, a ghostly owl hooted far up the valley, and the sun winked down out of sight. Then a fine rain started to fall. I stood there enthralled in the gathering gloom, my rod hooped and straining, the fisherman sunk in the ancient muck and ooze, ever so slowly fighting him up to the net. Give him line, take in line, come, darling, please come to daddy. . . . In ten ecstatic minutes—or was it years?—he lay gleaming in the net, as mistily colorful as a slice of rainbow robbed from the sky. Nearly a foot and a half in length he was, the loveliest native brook trout I had seen in many a year. And all this, believe it or not, within six miles of my own back yard!

It is seldom that rational men whistle when they must change a tire, especially in the rainy dark, but I know of one lunatic who did that night as he kept glancing up at the dripping creel of trout that sagged from the door of his car. . . . Since then my pal Henry and I have fished the old pond many times, but I must confess that never since have we found the trout as much on the prod as they were on that first magic night of rediscovery.

The unlikely old pond is truly enchanted; nowhere is it deeper than five feet, though the mud must go clean to Singapore. It crawls with bloodsuckers and the only fish in it are adult native brook trout. Even stranger, from opening day until about mid-season the place is teeming with trout; but along about the Fourth of July, as soon as the real summer heat comes along, they disappear as though someone had rung down a curtain or—worse yet—poisoned the pond overnight. The Lord only knows where or precisely why they go—but each spring at opening day they are back bigger and better than ever. There is a respectable inlet and a good outlet, and I keep promising myself that one day I must explore these unknown stretches, but my reason (sometimes the poorest of fishing guides) plus my aerial maps tell me there shouldn't be any decent open water anywhere near there. (But aerial maps can't show cool, deep, trouty beaver dams hidden away in the shade of enfolding trees.) At any rate, each year since then I give up the old puddle about mid-season and rattle off to other and greener pastures.

Perhaps next fall during bird or duck season I'll take my shotgun and my hip boots and explore the front and back doors of this queer old pond and try to discover where those smart trout go on their annual summer vacation. But perhaps that would spoil all the mystery of the pond; perhaps it is better to accept its favors humbly and without question; perhaps it is well to rest a lovely enchanted old pond that permits one to try for gallant and fighting native brook trout practically in one's own back yard.

Moral: Flat tire or no flat tire, pause once in a while in the summer madness of fishing; pause and take inventory and simply *make* yourself revisit some of those long-neglected and "fishless" old trout waters. There may be some big surprises in store. With me, at least, it has just about gotten so that my best and most exciting fishing is had at these forgotten old places that are totally ignored by those "smart" fishermen who day after day roar by them at top speed and, then, standing shoulder to shoulder like herd bulls, lash the more popular distant waters to a froth as foamy as an ad of their favorite beer.

8

Little Panama

My father, Nicholas Traver, was a tall man with big hands and the disposition of a bilious gnu. He was also the world's most successful saloonkeeper: that is, he hunted and fished all the time and only visited his saloon to raid the iron safe and cuss out the bartenders and lay in more hooch. He spent the rest of his time roaming the woods with his pal, old Dan McGinnis. Mostly he and Dan went to the favorite of his three camps, the South Camp.

Old Dan was a quick, wiry, mustached Scotch-Irish iron miner, turned trapper, who had violated the game laws so long and so well that they had finally given him a job and a star and called him a state trapper.

It was Dan's boast that he had never owned a game or fish license from the time, years before, when he had inadvertently stumbled into the county clerk's office and, not knowing just what else to do, had applied for a license. When the young man at the desk asked him the color of his eyes, he promptly replied, "Bloodshot," whereupon, Dan avowed, "the young whippersnapper commenced laffin' so hard he couldn't stop, so out I walks from the damn place, an' I ain't never been back. Of all the insultin' young bastards!"

Anyway, when Dan got to be a state trapper he was supposed to roam around the woods and trap wolves and coyotes and other predatory beasts; but when he got the star and the salary he quit trapping, and instead he and my father would go out to camp and fish and get a little drunk and play cards and argue.

My father and Dan would drive out of our back yard in the old buckboard with a barrel-bellied bay mare called Molly, the oats and a bale of hay in the back, a lantern clamped on the dashboard, and a battered water pail dangling from the rear axle. When they got to the gate my father, suddenly remembering, would call back to my mother. She would come hurrying out from the kitchen, wiping her hands on her apron, and quietly stand there on the back porch shading her eyes.

"We'll just be gone for the weekend, Bess," my father would say.

My mother would nod her head quickly and smile and wave her hand gladly, but sometimes when she turned away I noticed tears in her gray eyes. I guess it was because she knew that the weekend meant that she wouldn't see my father until the following Wednesday or Thursday, when they would return home for more food and whisky and beer, and then shortly depart once again "for the weekend."

But we boys said very little about my father being in the woods so much, because when he wasn't in the woods he was so crabby and bad-tempered that we wished he were. And he had two good bartenders, a Frenchman and a Cornishman, to run the saloon for him when he was gone. I have never in my life seen a man so crazy about the woods, about hunting and fishing, as my father. Unless it was old Dan McGinnis, the state trapper who wouldn't trap.

On my father's land there was a lake in which there were no fish. On the county map it was called Lake Traver, and I think my father was very proud of this—though he never spoke of it—because when they first came out with the big maps with Lake Traver on them, he stuck one on the wall of the saloon, above the music box, near a gaslight, and made a big circle around his lake with a red crayon.

Lake Traver was the only body of water on his land. It was a deep glacial jewel, with its steep rocky banks on one side, above which towered straight Norway pine trees, their fallen needles lying thick on the moss-covered old rocks and in the crevices. The rest of the shore line was mostly wild cranberry marsh, with young cherry trees and poplars and maples reaching back to the pines. The lake was spring-fed, gravel-bottomed, without an inlet, and the water was very clear. It was always cool, even in the middle of the summer. But there were no fish.

From season to season my father and old Dan had planted barrels of brook trout in the lake—trout fry, fingerlings, even mature trout—but they were never seen again. Old Dan once suggested, during a feverish argument over this phenomenon, that the real reason the trout didn't survive was because they couldn't live in a lake owned by such a cantankerous, poisonous old buzzard as my father. But my father pounded the table and shook his head and shouted, "I'll make the bastards live in there yet." So the next spring would see him and old Dan lurching and tugging and cursing more cans of doomed trout into Lake Traver.

The funny part of it was that all they had to do was to hike over on almost any of the next forties, owned by the lumber company, and there the streams and ponds and beaver dams abounded with trout.

Just over the line, on the lumber company's land, in sight of my father's lake, was a big ancient beaver dam teeming with brook trout. My father tried to buy the land with the big beaver dam on it, but the lumber company wouldn't sell because there was a nice stand of young white pine coming along on it. They told him he could fish the dam all he liked, and treat it as his own, but they would not sell. So my father, overcome with humility and profound gratitude, roared at them to go plumb to hell. "You graspin' capitalist bastards!" The gnawing horrors of Wall Street were always a favorite theme of my father's.

My father was an independent man. He was in fact one of the most independent men I ever knew. And stubborn, too. He got so mad because he couldn't buy the beaver dam that he ceased to fish on any of the lumber company's land. Since they owned all the land for miles around his camp, this left him only his fishless lake to fish in. And he dearly loved to fish.

He couldn't somehow bring himself to believe there were no trout in his lake, despite the fact that old Dan, who could catch fish in a desert, had tried all kinds of bait, had flung flies all over the lake, and had even netted and dynamited to test the place, but nary a fish.

It really got pretty bad. He and Dan would hitch up old Molly and plod morosely out to camp for the weekend, and by and by, after a few preliminary drinks, old Dan would sneak over to the beaver dam with his fishing tackle, and then in a little while my father, cursing quietly to himself, would slip through the woods to his lake. There they'd be, in plain sight of each other, old Dan landing one beautiful trout after the other out of the beaver pond, and my father, no longer cursing quietly to himself, circling and circling his lake like a crazed water buffalo, his long legs buried in the cranberry marshes, wallowing and threshing, fishing like mad, with never a solitary rise.

Later, when they met back at camp, old Dan would cock his head sideways, comb his mustache with his fingers, and say, all pert and bright, "Have any luck today, Nick?"

"Hell, no. No bloody luck. They ain't risin' today. The wind ain't right—but I guess it'll change by night, Danny."

Then old Dan would dig in the damp grass of his creel and lay out the trout he had caught, smiling and allowing that the wind wasn't so bad over his way. "Let's build us a damn good drink, Nick," Dan might add, licking his mustache.

"Yes, Dan, we had a pretty hard day." My father would be staring at Dan's trout.

"You better come fishing with me tonight over on the beaver dam, Nick."

"You go high-dive to hell, you trespassin' ol' rum-pot," my father would say, stomping into the camp.

I knew that all this was going on because occasionally my father and old Dan would take me along, "for a fishing trip," they called it. My fishing consisted mainly of taking care of the old mare, Molly, front and rear, weeding the stunted vegetable garden—which my father evidently maintained to vary the diet of rabbit and porcupine—and of paring potatoes, filling lamps, hauling water and firewood, and making up the bunks.

And then there was the business of mixing those whisky

sours for my father and Dan, which they never seemed to tire of. I learned to mix them before I learned to drink them. Whisky sours were one thing that my father and old Dan fully agreed upon. Never in my whole life have I seen two men who drank more whisky sours than my father and old Dan McGinnis.

It was on such a trip that the vision, the big solution, came to my father. It was a beautiful evening in the early spring, the trees were not yet in leaf, dusk was closing in, the whip-poorwills had started, the mists were rolling up from the marshes. I had finished doing the supper dishes and had put fresh salt on the deer licks. Dan and my father were out fishing, old Dan as usual over at his beaver dam, my father gloomily stalking his lake. I was just getting out the fixings for the whisky sours.

Suddenly I could hear them shouting out there in the twilight, and then their stomping, and they burst into the camp.

"By the roarin' Jesus, Nick, I think you got it—*a canal's the thing!* We'll run the bloody beaver dam over into your lake—an' that'll freshen and change the water, jus' like you say—hell, an'—why then there'll be oodles of trout livin' at last in Lake Traver. Well, I'll be cow-kicked!"

My father seldom got excited unless he was drunk or mad. This night he was neither, but he was very excited. His eyes were shining and I saw how he must have looked when he was a boy.

"It come to me sudden-like, Dan," he kept saying in an awed voice.

He kept illustrating and waving with sweeps of his big hands how they would scoop out the canal and join the beaver pond to the lake; how they would build stop dams at either end to keep out the water while they were digging.

64

"Why, Dan—listen, Dan—we'll tell that bloody lumber company crowd to go run up a hemp rope." Then turning to me: "Son, mix up a mess of whisky sours—take one for yourself." And then I got excited, too, because it was the first whisky sour I ever had. It was not the last—not even the last that night.

Although it was only Monday and the weekend was barely half over, early the next morning we hitched up protesting old Molly and hustled her back to town. My father and old Dan could talk of and plan nothing but the new canal.

After that we didn't see my father around the house for days—not for a good part of the summer, in fact. The very day we got home, he and Dan visited all the saloons in town, rounding up out-of-work lumberjacks and thirsty bar flies to help dig the canal.

They bought boxes and boxes of dynamite, got second-hand scrapers and picks and shovels, and third-hand horses, and paraphernalia galore. With their motley crew they threw up a cook-shack and bunk-house tent—and then rooted and gouged and slashed away at their canal all the summer through. The leaves were tinted and falling, the fishing season was nearly over, when they had finally dug their ditch from the beaver dam over to Lake Traver.

All summer long fishermen came from miles around to view the proceedings; to watch my father, stripped to the waist, a fanatic with a shovel, throwing up vast clouds of dirt, shouting, sweating, straining at rocks—and at the same time carefully, tenderly feeding his sad-eyed bar-fly crew just enough whisky to keep them from deserting and yet not enough so that they would tumble into the ditch. He was foreman, engineer, laborer, wet nurse and all the rest, rolled into one.

And old Dan—here, there, and everywhere, like a hornet

—cursing the teamsters, bullying the blasters, dispensing the drinks—occasionally falling into the ditch. But finally the great canal was dug and done and thirsting for water.

Labor Day was the big day, the grand opening. It seemed that half the town was lined up and down the big canal. My father had a bar set up along about the middle of the ditch. His two bartenders were there, aproned and sweating, working like mad serving free drinks. At noon my father got ready to fire his rifle, the signal for the blasters at each end of the canal to blow out the stop dams so that the prolific waters of the beaver pond would pour through the canal into the new trout paradise, Lake Traver.

As the noon hour drew near, everyone began to gravitate toward the middle of the canal. My father and old Dan stood out sort of in front of the rest, nearest the canal. Everybody was laughing and singing and talking.

Old Dan had a haircut and a red necktie for the occasion. He kept peering at a big silver watch and a soiled piece of paper which he held in his hand, clearing his throat. My father stood very tall and straight, his rifle ready in his hands. Then Dan raised his hand and glared at the crowd for silence. Squinting at the piece of paper which he held, he began to read, slowly and with dignity:

"This here is the dedication of Nick Traver's canal. We worked goddam hard on this here canal of Nick Traver's. You folks who is crazy about fishin' owe lots to the visions and leadership of my friend Nick Traver."

Dan turned to my father. "Let her go, Nick," he said, very quietly, and my father let her go, stepping back and handing the smoking rifle to me. Old Dan still stood peering at his watch. It took about half a minute for the short fuses to burn —the scampering blasters . . . and then two dull booms, practically together, and the stop dams were out. The hushed crowd pressed forward to the canal to watch.

For a moment nothing happened. Then we could hear a low rumbling roar, like distant thunder, growling and gathering; then we could see the water surging in from both directions in mighty waves, from the dam and from the lake, thundering, pounding, roaring and then—crash!—the two streams met in the middle of the canal, the ground trembled, and a great muddy wave burst high into the air, blotting out the sun like a typhoon, raining down all over—over Dan and my father, over me, the crowd, the bartenders, the whisky sours, over everything. And still the water roared in, hissing and boiling, while the dripping crowd stood there hunched and silent, like men at a lynching.

Then it happened. You could sense it before you could see it. There was an enormous flood of water coming from the lake, more and more and more, and then suddenly we saw —*we saw that the water was flowing in the wrong direction!* There was no mistake; it was roaring wildly past us from the lake into the beaver dam. We could see the dam rising and the lake lowering before our very eyes.

I looked at my father. He stood there dripping and mud-covered, shrunken-looking, his hair in his eyes, his mouth hanging open, watching the torrent pound into the beaver pond. Then we could see it before we could hear it, a cloud of earth and sticks and stones—it was war, a bombardment— then nothing but the pulsing surge of the water racing past us. And all the while my father and old Dan and the rest of us stood there, silently watching the fishless waters of Lake Traver emptying into the lumber company's ruined beaver dam. *The beaver dam had washed out.*

My father turned to me. He had closed his mouth. Looking like a little boy, he slowly wiped his muddy face with the back of his hand.

"Pa," I said very quietly, hoping the others would not hear. "Listen, Pa."

"What's that, son?"

"Pa, it looks like the whole trouble is your lake was higher than the beaver dam."

My father seemed to consider this. He pursed his lips and shook his head with little nods, thinking hard.

"Yes, son," he said finally, "it sure kind of looks that way."

Then someone tittered in the crowd. I heard it plainly. My father heard it too, for the look left his face in a flash, and he almost knocked me over as he leaped toward the crowd.

"*Who done that?*" he roared. "What dirty bastard done that?" He howled and danced before them, clutching out with his big hands, the veins standing out on his neck—a very bad sign. "I'll lick the hull mother-beating bunch of you!" he bellowed. The crowd gave ground as he advanced. "I don't give a rattlin' goddam for the hull snivelin' pack of you! I'll—"

Just then old Dan let out a whoop, and my father and everyone turned around just in time to see him sailing his big silver watch into the canal. He was acting like a drunken man in a beehive, leaping, laughing, cursing, shouting. He ran up to the boiling ditch, tore off his jacket, flung it in, turned and hollered, "Nick! Nick! It's a goddam swell idea—*a perfect swimmin' hole!*"

With that he took a mighty running dive, his thin legs crooked frog-fashion in the air, disappearing into the muddy water of the canal. My father and the rest frantically rushed up to save him. "Thar she blows!" someone hollered, just as old Dan came up spitting, snorting, splashing, looking like an aged walrus, threshing and trumpeting.

"Yoo hoo, boys!" he shouted, waving his hand. "Come on in—the water's fine!"

And, like the possessed swine of Gadara, every man jack of us, led by my father, went leaping pell-mell into what has been known, even to this day, as Nick Traver's Folly.

9

Paulson, Paulson, Everywhere

F o r many years I was district attorney of this bailiwick, and during that time I naturally had much to do with game wardens and, of course, with overzealous citizens who collided with the hunting and fishing laws. Indeed, I discovered some of my best fishing spots through these uneasy encounters; and while the following yarn is scarcely a fishing story, in any sporting sense, it *is* about trout and about some of the trout waters I found while plying my D. A. trade.

Up my way old township politicians never die; they merely look that way. Instead they become justices of the peace. It is a special Valhalla that townships reserve for their political cripples and has the following invariable rules of admission: The justice of the peace must be over seventy; he must be deaf; he must be entirely ignorant of any law but never admit it; and, during the course of each trial, he must chew—and violently expel the juice of—at least one (1) full package of Peerless tobacco. It is preferable that he speak practically no English, and that with an accent, but in emergencies an occasional exception is permitted to slip by. Sometimes I preferred the former.

I could write a lament as thick as this book about the grotesque experiences I have had trying justice court cases out before some of these rural legal giants. It is a depressing thought. Instead I shall tell you about the trial of Ole Paulson before Justice of the Peace Ole Paulson.

Ole Paulson of Nestoria township was charged with catching forty-seven brook trout out of season with a net. Ole Paulson was in rather a bad way because it is never legal to take or possess forty-seven brook trout in one day; to fish for them in any manner out of season; or ever to take brook trout with a net, in or out of season. Ole Paulson promptly pleaded not guilty and the case was set for trial before His Honor, Justice of the Peace Ole Paulson, also of Nestoria. I drove up there to try the case rather than send one of my assistants, not because I panted to sit at the feet of Justice Paulson, Heaven knows, but largely because I was dying to find out precisely where a man could ever *find* forty-seven brook trout in one place, regardless of how he took them. It was also a riotously beautiful September day, and afforded the D. A. a chance to escape from that personal prison he inhabits called his office.

"Vell, hayloo, Yonny!" His Honor greeted me as I entered his crowded courtroom, a high-ceilinged, plaster-falling, permanently gloomy establishment from which he ordinarily dispensed insurance of all kinds, assorted tourist supplies, game and fish licenses, live bait, not to mention various and sundry bottled goods and rubber accessories. "Ve vas yoost satting here vaiting for yew!"

"Was you, Your Honor?" I cackled gleefully, warming up disgracefully to this local political sachem, pumping his limp hand, inquiring about his rheumatism—or was it his flaring ulcers?—respectfully solicitous over his interminable replies, making all the fuss and bother over him that both he and the villagers demanded whenever the District Attorney came to town to attend court. It was understood that we two initiates into the subtle mysteries of the law had to put on a show for the groundlings. . . . The courtroom was crowded, every adult male in the community having somehow gathered enough energy to forsake the village tavern for a few hours and move across the street for the trial.

I turned to the People's star witness, the eager young game warden who had arrested the defendant. "Is the jury chosen yet?" I asked him in a stage whisper that must have been audible to a farmer doing his fall plowing in the next township. There could be no sneaky professional secrets in Judge Paulson's court—the penalty was swift and sure defeat.

"Yes," the game warden answered, "I struck the jury this morning. The list of jurors was prepared by Deputy Sheriff Paulson here. The six jurors are all here now."

It had not escaped my notice that I seemed to be getting fairly well hemmed in by Paulsons, but it was a trifle late to get into that now. I'd have to trust to the Lord and a fast outfield. I turned to Justice Paulson and said: "Very well, Your Honor, the People are ready to proceed with the trial."

"Okay den," His Honor said, rapping his desk with a gavel ingeniously contrived from a hammer wrapped in an old sock. He pointed to six empty chairs against a far wall. "Yantlemen of da yury," he announced, "yew vill now go sat over dare." Six assorted local characters scrambled for their seats, relaxed with a sigh, and were duly sworn by Justice Paulson. Allowing the jurors to sit for the oath was only one of his minor judicial innovations.

Justice Paulson, exhausted by administering the oath, opened a fresh package of Peerless and stowed away an enormous chew in his cheek. There was a prolonged judicial pause while he slowly worked up this charge. He spat a preliminary stream against a tall brass cuspidor. "*Spa-n-n-n-g!*" rang this beacon, clanging and quivering like an oriental summons to evening prayer. "Okay," His Honor said in a Peerless-muffled voice.

"The People will call Conservation Officer Clark," I announced, and the eager young game warden arose, was sworn, took the stand—and told how he had come upon the defendent, Ole Paulson, lifting the net from Nestoria creek just below the second beaver dam in Section 9. "I caught him red-handed," he added.

"Do you have the trout and the net?" I asked the young warden, slyly noting the latitude and longitude of this fabulous spot.

"Oh, yes," he answered. "The net is in my car outside— and the trout are temporarily in the icebox in the tavern across the street. Is it okay if I go over and get them now?"

I turned to His Honor, "Your Honor, the People request a five-minute recess," I said.

Judge Paulson, moon-faced and entirely mute now from his expanding chew of Peerless, whanged another ringer, banged his homemade gavel on his desk and, thus unpouched, managed to make his ruling. "Yentlemen, Ay declare fi'-minoot intermissin so dat dis hare young conversation feller kin go gat his fish." He turned to a purple and bladdery bystander. "Sharley," he said, "go along vit him over an' unlock da tavern."

I gnawed restlessly on an Italian cigar while Charlie, the tavern owner and my sole witness, went across the street to fetch the evidence. The jury sat and stared at me in stolid silence. His Honor replenished his chew, like a starved Italian hand-stoking spaghetti. "*Whing!*" went the judge, every minute on the minute. A passing dog barked. The bark possessed a curious Swedish accent, not "woof" but "*weuf*"! I wondered idly whether "Sharley" and my man had got locked in a pinochle match when lo! they were back, the flushed tavern keeper appreciatively licking his moist chops over the unexpected alcoholic dividend he had been able to spear. The jury watched him closely, to a man corroded with envy. The young officer placed the confiscated net and a dishpan full of beautiful frozen brook trout on the judge's desk and resumed the witness chair.

"Officer, you may state whether or not this is the net you found the defendant lifting from Nestoria creek on the day in question?" I asked, pointing.

"It is," the officer testified.

Pointing at the fish: "And were all these fish the brook trout you removed from the net?"

"They were."

"Were the fish then living?"

"About half. But they were nearly done in. None would have survived."

"How many are there in the pan?"

"Forty-seven."

I introduced the exhibits into evidence and turned to Judge Paulson. "The People rest," I said.

"*Plink!*" acknowledged Judge Paulson, turning to the defendant. "Da defandant vill now race his right han' an' tell da yury *hiss* side of da story." It was not a request.

Ole Paulson was sworn and testified that it was indeed he who had been caught lifting the writhing net; that he had merely been patrolling the creek looking for beaver signs for the next trapping season when he had come across the illegal net; that the net was not his and was not set by him; and that he was just lifting the net to free the unfortunate trout and destroy the net when, small world, the conservation officer had come along and arrested him for his humanitarian pains. "Dat's all dare vere to it!" he concluded.

I badgered and toyed with the witness for several minutes, but it was an unseasonably hot September day and I could see that the fans were anxious to get back across the street to their hot pinochle games and cool beer, so I cut my cross-examination short. In my brief jury argument I pointed out the absurdity of the defendant's story that he was out prowling a trout stream in mid-September looking for beaver signs for a trapping season that opened the following March. I also briefly gave my standard argument that every time a game violator did things like this he was really no different from a thief stealing the people's tax money— that the fish and game belonged to *all* the people. . . . The members of the jury blinked impassively over such strange political heresy.

"S-*splank!*" went Judge Paulson, scoring another bull's-eye. Had any man moved carelessly into the crossfire he would have risked inundation and possible drowning.

The defendant's argument was even briefer than mine. "Yantleman of da yury," he said, rising and pointing scornfully at the fish net. "Who da hecks ever caught a gude Svede using vun of dem gol-dang homemade Finlander nets? *Ay tank you!*" He sat down.

"B-blink!" went the Judge, banishing the jury to the back room to consider their verdict.

The jury was thirstier than I thought. "Ve find da defandant *note gueelty!*" the foreman gleefully announced, two minutes later.

"Whang!" rang the cuspidor, accepting and celebrating the verdict.

After the crowd had surged tavernward, remarkably without casualty, I glanced over the six-man jury list, moved by sheer morbid curiosity. This was the list:

Ragnar Paulson
Swan Paulson
Luther Paulson
Eskil Paulson
Incher Paulson
Magnus Carl Magnuson

I turned to Deputy Sheriff Paulson. "How," I asked sternly, "how did this ringer Magnuson ever get on this jury list?"

Deputy Paulson shrugged. "Ve yust samply ran out of Paulsons," he apologized. "Anyvay, Magnuson dare vere my son's brudder-in-law. My son vere da defandant, yew know!"

"Spang!" gonged His Honor, like a benediction. "Dat vere true, Yonny," he said. "My nephew dare—da deputy sheriff— he nefer tell a lie!"

I lurched foggily across the street and banged on the bar. "Drinks fer da house!" I ordered, suddenly going native. "Giff all da Paulsons in da place vatever dey vant!"

10

The Haunted Pond

WHEN I was a kid there were no bass or German browns in our lakes and streams and, as nearly as I can recall, few if any rainbows. When a man said he was going fishing he meant he was going fishing for brook trout. Our waters were loaded with them. Then along came the bass. The advent of these sea monsters was greeted with shouts of wild delight by the bored native fishermen; here at last was *really* a big fighting fish; and soon throngs of sleepy fishermen were up all hours of the night greeting overdue trains, gaily acquiring assorted calluses and hernias as they unloaded can after can of wriggling government bass fry and fingerlings into waiting buckboards and Model-T Fords and rushed them out and dumped them into our lovely trout waters. It still makes me shudder to contemplate the fumbling midnight horror of this picture.

Needless to say, most of these fishermen lived to regret

their hot haste; and again needless to say, much of our good trout water was permanently usurped by the bass and eventually ruined for *all* fishing. It is only in comparatively recent years that state-directed poisoning programs have removed the bass from some of our natural trout ponds and lakes and retrieved these waters for the fish that really belong there. The bass-infested trout rivers and streams present another and more difficult problem, but in general it is perhaps fair to say that nature saw to it that the bass soon died out or became a negligible factor in the true trout streams, while those streams and rivers in which the bass have thrived were probably doomed as trout waters anyway.

I personally don't happen to care a whoop for bass fishing or bass; in fact I loathe it and them; but I have no quarrel with the queer people who do, only a sort of bewildered pity. My big gripe is that I believe bass should be confined to bass waters, and I weep and grit my teeth and see red when I find the ugly brutes fouling up and crowding out our vanishing trout waters.

The point is that for their own scaly sakes bass should not be planted in trout waters; they not only ruin the water for trout, but they themselves are ultimately doomed. It is now known that bass will thrive in these trout waters for the first few years, growing to huge and awesome dimensions, but by and by, after all of the rough natural food is consumed, they will inevitably languish and grow stunted so that nobody is happy, not even the dwarfed bass.

Alas, my own father was guilty of more than his share of planting bass in our trout waters. He lived to regret it and I have forgiven him much in this respect, but I have never rightly forgiven him for planting bass in the lovely natural trout waters we used to fish.

One spring my father got authentic reports that the Winthrop boys had been winter-fishing the brook trout out at
old Blair pond. "Aha, I'll fix 'em," my father said, so he and
my older brother Leo quick got a load of bass and dumped
them into the pond. (Bass mud down in the winter in a
kind of quasi-dormant stupor and cannot readily be caught,
at least up in this part of the state where winter doesn't
fool.) At the time I did not know anything about this ter-
rible deed, but it would not have done any good if I had
because my father was not the kind of man who discussed
his decisions with any man; he simply announced them.

My father indeed thwarted the Winthrop boys, all right,
but it was a clear case of cutting off his nose to spite his face,
because in two years not a single trout could be taken from
the pond and after that it began to yield up the biggest
and ugliest bass it has ever been my displeasure to look in
the eye. For several years I used to lure bass fishermen out
there with their chests of hardware in a vain hope that they
might somehow fish the devilish monsters out. Many huge
bass were winched in, and by and by they did disappear,
only to be replaced by a race of midgets; and it shortly got
so that one could take a mature undersized bass on nearly
every cast, so stunted and hungry had they grown. At last I
realized that the old place had been permanently ruined
for all fishing. I nearly wept.

I should like to digress here and comment briefly on the
various theories that account for what it is that makes trout
disappear when bass take over their waters. For disappear
they certainly do. One simple theory is that the bass eat all
the trout (except for the very largest trout, who ultimately
roll their eyes and die of loneliness); another that the trout
perish of internal flat tires from eating the tiny spike-backed
bass fry; another that the bass starve out the trout by their

swinish consumption of all available food. And there are doubtless other theories. I rather lean to the first theory, but I am willing to concede that the other things are probably contributing factors.

The only places I have ever seen bass and trout persist together are in those waters where the trout have an opportunity to get away from the bass to spawn and get their growth before they come back down to vie with the bass. Lorraine Lake in this county (with its various springs and deeps and shallows—and many inlets) is such a spot; all of which rather lends force to the theory that it is the bass eating the smaller trout that causes the latter's ultimate extinction and not the trout fatally eating the smaller bass. But to get back to my haunted and ruined pond.

Along about the summer of 1940, perhaps fifteen years after the bass were planted, I first met Dr. Albert Hazzard. He was and is director of the institute for fisheries research, a branch of the division of fisheries of the Michigan conservation department working in co-operation with the state university at Ann Arbor. Doc Hazzard is not only a scientifically trained fish man and a good one but, I soon discovered, a swell modest guy to boot. I cornered him and chokingly told him the sad and harrowing tale of Blair Pond. He said he'd like to look at the place as the state was keenly interested in reclaiming all and any good trout waters for public trout fishing. I quick glanced at my watch and said when.

One way and another it was the summer of 1941 before Doc and his boys got out to Blair Pond. They did their stuff —caught bass, tested for plankton and other food content, took temperatures, etc.—and the upshot was that Doc wrote me that while the bass were both stunted and diseased, the pond was "highly suitable for trout," a conclusion which did not astound me since I had caught scores of speckled beauties out of it when I was a kid. Doc went on to say that they would not be able to make their poison survey until the following August, following which they could then poison out the bass and restock with trout within a month or so. He wound up his letter with these magic words: ". . . and there should be some trout fishing as early as 1943." I let out a whoop and turned three handsprings and went fishing.

Then along came Pearl Harbor, which unsettled more than fishermen, and I was not surprised when Doc wrote me the following June that the government had frozen all stocks of fish poison (rotenone) for the duration. However, there was one note of hope: Doc promised to complete the survey that summer so that the pond would at least be up near the top of the list when and if the stuff again became available. Thus were the villainous bass reprieved until the war ended.

In the autumn of 1946 Doc's boys (now mostly ex-G. I.'s) marched back and poisoned out the pond, but it developed that the first post-war poison released to the state was far too weak, and everything but a few minnows managed to weather the Borgia blitz. The thing was necessarily put off until the following year. In 1947 the question of poisoning out the pond struck a new snag over the further question of public access to the pond, once it was poisoned out and re-stocked. The objection was most reasonable so I swallowed my disappointment and cheerfully helped Doc and the conservation department to clear up this snag. Then in 1948, lo and behold, Doc's boys came and re-poisoned the pond and restocked it with nice clean little trout. At long last the thing was done.

I deliberately avoided the place until the 1950 season and I can best summarize the situation I then found by quoting from a letter I wrote Doc:

Trout Madness

You will be interested to receive a progress report on Blair Pond. I fished it this year for the first time since the planting. The first time I fished it I found both dams in good shape and the water well up. There were no rises and a short interval of worm fishing produced nothing. Last Saturday I tried it again with flies, spinning lures and finally, in desperation, with worms. Sitting on the rock part of the dam on the lower pond my partner finally got a good bite but missed the strike. Hearing his shout I joined him from the upper pond and threw in my porkchop and got a good bite and hooked the fish. It was an 11-inch brook trout full of fight and unusually heavy for its length. I would say it went three-quarters of a pound and was very "deep-chested" and literally hump-backed with flesh. There was no evidence of lice in the gills. A few minutes later my partner hooked and landed a slightly larger brook trout, and a few minutes later while retrieving my hook a heavy trout nailed the almost bare hook and after a splendid fight (I was using a bare fly hook, fine leader and fly rod) I landed a beautiful brook trout that went exactly 13 inches and was as plump as a partridge and must have weighed a pound and a half, most unusual for a trout that length.

Yesterday I returned with 2 friends. There was a high wind which made fishing difficult and we finally settled down to worms. Right off the bat we caught 2 trout, both about 11 inches and both unusually plump and full of fight. The flesh was salmon pink on all the trout. We saw no rises although both days should have produced rises towards evening. Yesterday we caught 3 shiners, and I can only conclude that they worked up over the bottom dam or else came out of some slough above. The beaver had dammed one of the two small inlets, one of the dams being practically at the edge of the lake and I am wondering if this will interfere with spawning.

We saw literally hundreds of minnows from an inch and a half to two inches but were unable to catch any although we chose to think they looked and behaved like trout fry. I am simply delighted with the way the trout appear to have taken hold although I am a little puzzled by the lack of rises. If you or your boys are up this way this summer I think it would be interesting to do a little seining to see how many survived the original planting. Certainly those that did are in excellent shape and there is every evidence that they will be propagating.

Little did I realize that I was whistling my way past the cemetery.

Doc replied, thanking me for my report and stating that he was "disturbed" by my report of the small minnows, as he suspected that they were young chubs or shiners and not trout fry. Following the 1950 trout season I wrote Doc partly as follows:

The place now has me baffled. In May, as I wrote you, we took five beautiful fat brooks, 11 to 13 inches, but all on bait. During the summer I haunted the place and never took or saw another trout—on bait or otherwise. There are hundreds of what we call shiners. The place is loaded with them. I did not see a single authentic trout rise. I fished late and early, on the surface and on the bottom and in between. In July we hauled a boat in there and scoured the place. Surface temperatures averaged 70 degrees. This occurred after a comparatively warm spell. We could not locate, from surface temperatures, the springs you once found during your surveys.

I am afraid the place may be one of those early and late season places, but the thing that dismays me most is my inability to see or attract a trout at or near the surface. Bait fishing leaves me cold. . . . If you get up here next summer I hope you and I can go and take a look. The boat is still there —and few fishermen appear to have been near the place. If we hadn't caught those five beauties I'd swear there were no trout in there.

Doc wrote back that he would personally make a check in the summer of 1951. This we did—and our nets showed that the ponds were infested with hundreds of chubs, shiners and suckers—but nary a trout. Doc concluded that the rough fish had survived and come in from tiny spring feeders above. That fall Doc's boys again poisoned out the ponds—and all feeders—and not a single trout showed up. *We had caught the only 5 trout that survived the 1948 planting of several thousand fish!* By then I was about ready for the gas pipe—but I reckoned without Doc Hazzard.

The pond was again poisoned out and replanted in the spring—a monument to the persistence and vision of Doc Hazzard. I have resolved not to fish there for several years —and then—so help me, following the first trout I take on a fly I swear I'll swallow a fifth of Old Cordwood and jump in with my clothes on. For that will be a day. And I wish my old bass-loving father could be there to see it.

11

Crystal-Ball Fishing

IN THE watery and spectral half-world inhabited by trout fishermen there dwell many fanatic sects,
each with its own stout band of followers, and each claim-
ing exclusive possession of the one true ladder to trout
heaven. At one time or another I have tarried with most of
these sects and dallied with their doctrine: the disciples of
lunar tables, the pilgrims who yield only to barometric
pressures, the worshipers at the shrines of tidal impulses,
wind directions, thermal dynamics, water strata, sun spots,
spots before the eyes—and all the others. Then one day there
came the light, and I became a lamb strayed from the fold,
a renegade and a blasphemer. For I now embrace the heresy
that the "best" time to go fishing is when you can get away.
I have also concluded that Dr. Bile's Almanac (for 1911) is
about as good a fishing guide as all the involved scientific
claptrap with which so many present-day fishermen clutter
their comings and goings.

Trout Madness

There is not the slightest doubt, of course, that the fishing is better on some days than it is on others, and that frequently certain parts of the day are better than others. All fishermen know that. My thesis is that I do not believe anyone can predict those times—at least for any appreciable period in advance—, and it both amuses and irks me to watch certain self-appointed native witch doctors blandly arrogate this authority to themselves. Any dolt with a head full of Crisco may suspect that the fishing *might* be lousy when he sets forth in the teeth of a belting northeast gale, with the barometers crashing all about him, but I am talking about those smug gentry who sit in skyscrapers in January and undertake to tell me what the fishing will be on Herkimer's Pond at 4:42 P.M. the following July 17. I just can't buy it and I'll try to tell you why.

The big trouble with all these trout swamis, in my book, is that they try to select and blow up one of the many admittedly important fishing *factors* into an exclusive revealed religion; that as a class they incline to ignore the fact that there are many variable factors that combine endlessly to influence trout fishing; and, perhaps most serious, that they tend to forget that even when all known factors are isolated and weighed and calibrated, that the unknown factors ever lurking in the weeds are likely as not to pop up and throw all their fine calculations into a tailspin.

If one must get into the act and couch this ill-natured swipe at the high priests of fishing in the argot of science, I'll venture to put it this way: mathematicians have not yet found a way to solve a problem when the necessary factors X and Y are unknown. That, I believe, is unassailably sound scientific doctrine. And it is my further belief that this maxim applies equally to fishing, and that it is a rare time when we go fishing that, at the very least, fish factors X and Y are not only unknown but often totally unsuspected. I realize I'm drifting boldly into the realm of fish mysticism, but I further suspect that usually these unknown factors embrace a good part of the entire fishing alphabet. There is so incredibly much that all men, let alone we little fishermen, don't know and perhaps can't ever know.

I'll attempt to give just one example. Over a long period of years I have observed a certain strange fishing phenomenon—and one that I have yet to see mentioned or even hinted at in all the scores of fishing treatises and assorted revelations I have read. It is this: On some days the surface of the water possesses a peculiar gun-metal sheen, a kind of bland, polished, and impersonal glitter, a most curious sort of bulging look, coupled with the aloof, metallic quality and cold, glassy expression of a dowager staring down a peasant through her lorgnette. At the same time there is a deceitful appearance of warmth, an opaque expression of bland geniality, and the light reflects off the water in a curiously false-friendly way. It is all very subtle and confusing and hard to describe, yet when I see it I never for an instant mistake it. On such days, fortunately rare, I have learned that I might just as well leave my rod in the case and instead go chase butterflies or lurking girl-scout leaders.

Please don't ask me what all this means or why it is so or what causes it. I have seen it on the high barometer and the low; at the time of the full moon, the half moon and no moon at all; and at times when the swamis had predicted good fishing, medium fishing—or had even flatly recommended staying home and mowing the front lawn. In fact this strange phenomenon seems to have no discernible connection with any of the current theories of the Learned Society of Elder Swamis. I have come to sense dimly that it is simply one of the unknown factors of which I speak—or perhaps, more accurately, an end result or observable symptom of one or more of these unknown factors.

But there it is and when "it" is there the fishing is invariably lousy. If you want me to speculate about this and play a little at being a crystal-ball gazer myself, I'd *guess* that it may be simply that the unusual lighting somehow makes the fish wary and more easily seen by their natural foes, so that they sulk in their cyclone cellars. Or perhaps the peculiar lighting affects their eyes. Or perhaps their appetites. Or perhaps—but you see where we land when we thus try to penetrate the great fishing unknown? And the only way I can tell when "it" is there is to go look at the water. When it is present it seems to visit its blight indifferently upon all waters in the vicinity.

I suppose I could parley all this into quite an impressive fish religion, and perhaps even start a new sect. I do not intend to. For my part I'd rather spend my time in fishing than in missionary wooing of superstitious and gullible fishermen. It is bad enough for me to have to see it and sigh and shrug and open a can of beer and hope, usually vainly, that it will go away. Yet none of the official fish guessers seem ever to have seen or heard of it, let alone to have weighed or accounted for it when issuing their edicts. Nevertheless it is my opinion that this occurrence is simply a reflection of one of the many and infinitely varied unknown factors that constantly influence fishing (and doubtless many other things); factors that also just as constantly damn and ruin the "scientific" validity of all the incantations I have mentioned.

The more one fishes for trout, then, the more he is forced to the conclusion that no man knows even faintly when or why the fishing will be good or bad. Too often have all of us marched forth hopefully on those rare "perfect" days—

when all the licensed fish prophets were for once smiling and nodding in sweet accord—only to return wondering whether all the trout hadn't migrated to Mars. Or again, too often have we braved their collective frowns—and gone out and hit the jackpot. *Why?* I don't know why, otherwise I would set up shop as a swami myself—and henceforth tramp the trout circuits of the world, fishing away like mad on the proceeds of my sage revelations.

While we indeed live in an advanced age of science, and an alarming one at that, many men are too apt to think that therefore *all* the problems of living—and fishing—can be solved by applying the pragmatic methods of science to problems that are perhaps essentially insoluble. The same men laugh at the superstitions of our quaint ancestors and at the leaping witch doctors of present-day primitive tribes, yet themselves gladly swallow enough phony science every day to make even the dizziest witch doctor look like Dr. Einstein.

I hasten to add that most trout swamis are a serious, well-intentioned, and dedicated crew who genuinely love to fish; they are often highly intelligent men, perhaps lacking only in the saving perspective offered by a sense of humility and humor, whose pretensions after all cause little harm and possibly save quite a few trout. In a sense they are victims of their own hobbies. And sometimes their predictions are dead right, as they are occasionally bound to be, like a man who always plays the same number in roulette. They can't possibly always be wrong. Their occasional home runs are in fact the thing that keeps them in business.

There's one other thing that helps weld their flocks together. If, rightly or wrongly, a disciple of one of these fanatic fishing faiths *believes* that the fishing is going to be good, in that frame of mind he is naturally going to fish better—and that, too, is still a pretty important factor in all fishing. And should his favorite prophet say nay, the more devoted disciple generally doesn't even dare go fishing, so he is scarcely in a position to convict let alone accuse his holy man of treasonable error. Or if he goes fishing anyway, possibly because he has already planned the trip, his heart isn't in it, he is oppressed by a sense of sin for slumming among the heathen, his decalogue is shattered. One way or another he is less likely to be on the ball. Consequently he is apt to ascribe his subsequent fishing pratfall as still another triumph for his particular fishing saint. Thus, you see, his favorite prophet simply can't lose.

It's the same sort of thing as the fisherman and his "favorite" fly. The fly became a favorite, of course, because he or a pal once caught or raised a lot of trout with it; therefore he has faith in it, it is a "good" fly; therefore he fishes it more often and with greater care; therefore he is more likely to continue to take most of his fish on it; and therefore, to complete the vicious circle, he becomes more and more caught in the spell of his favorite fly. Or even take a strange deluded fellow who becomes depresssed when he thinks he sees a certain mysterious gun-metal sheen on the water. . . .

For my part it will be a sorry day when any character can ever tell me ahead of time what my fishing is going to be. To me the indescribable sense of anticipation and mystery in simply *going* fishing is almost half the fun. It is the beckoning lure of the unknown, the very unpredictability of the enterprise, that draws me on and on. Always I keep telling myself: This may be the big day when I'll get on—and stay on—to Grampaw. . . . And if ever some sly superswami comes along who can *really* tell me what I'm apt to do on Frenchman's Pond tomorrow night, he'd better quick gather up his crystal ball and start running. And he'd better not trip on his robes. Because I'm going to crack him and his crystal ball with my stoutest trout priest. I've now given him fair warning.

Have I told you my own new pet theory, the one about the influence of *bald spots* on trout fishing? Boy oh boy, it never fails! It's terrific! Oh, so you don't want to hear about it? So you prefer to worship at that eccentric rival angling church across the street—the one with bats in its belfry? Very well and *pardon* me. If you still want to blindly embrace such a weird collection of medieval fishing dogma and superstition, hop to it. See if I care. It's a free country. But as for me, *I'll* still cling to my precious bald spots. Because, you see, bald spots are milder. And, lordy, how they do satisfy!

12

Trout Heaven

THERE is a certain bass lake in these parts the water height of which is regulated by the whims of nature coupled with the variable needs of a certain incorporated benevolence known as an hydroelectric company. Since both parties are strangely uncommunicative and their moods are equally unpredictable, it is difficult for me to tell ahead of time just when the damn place will be ripe for fishing. I'm just not consulted. . . . But why, you may ask, why does this prideful fellow who dilates so interminably on being a trout-fishing purist—why should this untouchable take the slightest interest in waters inhabited by the miserable and lowly *bass*?

The reason, my friends, is that I am a member of a small secretive band of fishermen that knows that this so-called "bass" lake is also inhabited by trout—what is more, by big, savage, lantern-jawed, square-tailed, native brook trout! The gimmick—and the cross we must bear—is that one has a fighting chance to take these trout on flies *only* during those rare periods when the lake level is way down low. When that happens the usually flooded and submerged channel of a certain inlet becomes exposed; the banks become dried out; the mechanical aspects of fly-casting are then ideal; and for some mysterious reason that still baffles me—doubtless connected with food, temperatures, and protection—the big trout then come crowding pell-mell into this enchanted half-mile-long exposed channel in incredible numbers. Verily, it is so.

My theory is that as the lake waters continue to recede and the competition for food daily grows more keen, the trout perforce leave the cool deeps (where I suspect they normally dwell) and range out not only in search of food but also to avoid the ever-narrowing proximity with the bass. (You see, even the trout hate 'em!) I also suspect that as the waters dwindle the lake temperatures doubtless rise, and the sensitive trout, with their low toleration for rising temperatures, come crowding into the old river outlet to enjoy the concentrated coolness of fresh aerated waters pouring out of the deep woods. At any rate one thing is certain: given these conditions, the trout are *there;* and while the anguished and threadbare utility people prostrate themselves and beat their breasts and burn incense daily for rain, our little knot of initiated trout fishermen smile evilly and quietly foregather from miles around. For then it is we know that we are about to enter the very front door of trout heaven.

According to my fish records the last time Lake Enchantment (don't ever go *looking* for a lake of that name!) was "right" was back in mid-July, 1946. My entries for that period are faintly incredible. Here is an early and typical one:

Tommy Cole, Pinky Strand, Raymond Friend and I outboarded up to the main inlet early this morning. What a wildly beautiful Canadian-type lake to be wasted on bass—with the tall balsams and spruces pressing right down to the normal shore line and with the brooding dark hills sweeping beyond. A magnificent buck in velvet stood on a wind-swept open point and disdainfully watched us out of sight, as motionless as an iron deer on a lawn. Four men in a stuttering and smelly boat weren't going to budge *him* from his mosquito-free haven. . . .

Weather cloudy and rather coolish. Barometer off but holding steady. Rather brisk northwesterly winds. Approaching the channel had to lift motor and paddle rest of way. Tommy sculls a paddle beautifully—even in this old scow. Deadheads everywhere, some big enough to stove the *Queen Mary*. Around noon made tea and lunched. Mysterious inky water now down a foot below top of banks of the winding old channel. Banks getting fairly dry except for few side pools and puddles. No rises. Saw two bald eagles sweeping and tacking far overhead, an incredibly graceful and lovely sight. Sometimes wish I were a little bald eagle instead of merely a little bald. . . . This desolate place, with the rigid crazily twisted limbs of the long-engulfed dead trees reaching witch-fingered in the air, looks like a deserted street in Hell.

Still no rises, Raymond busily gathering clam shells. Must be planning on renewing barter with the Indians. I house-cleaned through my disordered fly boxes. Lordy, I carry enough flies to start a store. . . . It was around 5:00 when Tommy, doggedly casting blind with his own favorite Cole Special, a wet hair fly, pricked and rolled a tremendous trout. I swear I heard it growl. . . . First action of the day! *On the very next cast* the same fish hit again, in a maddened lunge, and this time Tommy was on to him, obliviously dancing his big-fish adagio, like he does, and chanting "Where oh where can my little dog be?" In less than ten minutes of superb handling he had nearly four pounds of copped dynamite folded and sagging in his net. He gave us a little sidelong glance. "The name is Cole, men," he said.

All of us then leapt to work except Raymond—who doesn't

fish, strange man—and then the real rise suddenly started! I had on a 14 Adams dry, but I believe they would have taken a red wig. The thing was incredible. Big mantelpiece trout obliviously flopping and rolling all around us, like suckers on a spawning run. They battled each other for our flies. There were few intervals when at least one of us wasn't on to a trout, and at one time I know all three of us—foolishly less than 100 feet apart—were on to tackle-busters at the same time. I lost mine, a real sleigh-dog of a trout, on a submerged deadhead trying craftily to move him down away from the others. Innocence is the best policy . . . Raymond let out an anguished Tarzan whoop in my ear. "You *lost* him," he said in an awed voice. I nodded grimly and wrapped on the first fly I could grab. It happened to be a Grizzly King the size of a pregnant mouse. I then proceeded to lose three different flies in a row to three other soakers on the strike—always and forever my biggest and most persistent fishing headache, especially under pressure. That, plus my insistence on using fine leaders.

In thirty minutes the rise ended as abruptly as it began. I was so weak I had to sit down, like the time when I chased and caught that fat boy who broke our window on Halloween. Box score: Tommy, 5 brook trout from 2 to 4 pounds; Pinky, 4 from 1 to 3 pounds; clumsy me, 2 measly fingerlings of about 1½ pounds each. . . . It was one of the fiercest, most thrilling and memorable jags of trout fishing I have ever been on anywhere. What a mad half-hour! That night in the gathering dusk as we nosed the boat quietly down through the maze of whale-sized deadheads, Tommy burst into song: "With his tail cut short and his hair cut long, where oh where can he be!" All joined in. The startled eagles drifted out from their pine-clad hills, the better to observe our dementia.

That magic year this sort of fabled fishing lasted nearly a month—until finally the prayers of the utility folks were answered, and a three-day young cloudburst hit us in early August. We were almost relieved that the fantasy was over; the fishing—and domestic—strain was beginning to tell. The

place gave us nearly every fishing experience in the book—
and a few I'd never heard of. Some days there was no rise
and no fishing; some days there was no rise and good fishing; some days a good rise and good fishing; and some days
a good rise and no fishing. Other days there was a little of
everything. And on a few days the fishing was simply fantastic. Most of these just bore down and headed out into the
lake till something gave way. I firmly believe that Doc
Thomas' old record could be smashed in this place—that is,
if a man could ever hold a record trout in all those deadheads.

While I'm in the grip of confession (I'll probably be
drummed out of the lodge for this) I'll tell you another secret.
Here it's only mid-March and there's practically no snow
left in the woods. The spring runoff is nearly over. Extremely
low water is plainly indicated. The graybeards predict a
long drought this summer. As for this fisherman, I'm busily
laying in some heavier leaders. (When the pinch comes I
probably won't use 'em.) And in the meantime I intend re-
ligiously to practice the difficult art of the sure but gentle
strike. For it looks as if the tattered utility people are about
to go into another long pout as we patient fisherfolk once
again stand expectantly on the threshold of trout heaven.
And this time I'm locking up my office and pitching a tent.
Watch out, Doc Thomas, here we come!

13

The Intruder

IT WAS about noon when I put down my fly rod and sculled the little cedar boat with one hand and ate a sandwich and drank a can of beer with the other, just floating and enjoying the ride down the beautiful broad main Escanaba River. Between times I watched the merest speck of an eagle tacking and endlessly wheeling far up in the cloudless sky. Perhaps he was stalking my sandwich or even, dark thought, stalking me. . . . The fishing so far had been poor; the good trout simply weren't rising. I rounded a slow double bend, with high gravel banks on either side, and there stood a lone fisherman—the first person I had seen in hours. He was standing astride a little feeder creek on a gravel point on the left downstream side, fast to a good fish, his glistening rod hooped and straining, the line taut, the leader vibrating and sawing the water, the fish itself boring far down out of sight.

Trout Madness

Since I was curious to watch a good battle and anxious not to interfere, I eased the claw anchor over the stern— *plop*—and the little boat hung there, gurgling and swaying from side to side in the slow deep current. The young fisherman either did not hear me or, hearing, and being a good one, kept his mind on his work. As I sat watching he shifted the rod to his left hand, shaking out his right wrist as though it were asleep, so I knew then that the fight had been a long one and that this fish was no midget. The young fisherman fumbled in his shirt and produced a cigarette and lighter and lit up, a real cool character. The fish made a sudden long downstream run and the fisherman raced after him, prancing through the water like a yearling buck, gradually coaxing and working him back up to the deeper slow water across from the gravel bar. It was a nice job of handling and I wanted to cheer. Instead I coughed discreetly and he glanced quickly upstream and saw me.

"Hi," he said pleasantly, turning his attention back to his fish.

"Hi," I answered.

"How's luck?" he said, still concentrating.

"Fairish," I said. "But I haven't raised anything quite like you seem to be on to. How you been doin'—otherwise, I mean?"

"Fairish," he said. "This is the third good trout in this same stretch—all about the same size."

"My, my," I murmured, thinking ruefully of the half-dozen-odd barely legal brook trout frying away in my sun-baked creel. "Guess I've just been out floating over the good spots."

"Pleasant day for a ride, though," he said, frowning intently at his fish.

"Delightful," I said wryly, taking a slow swallow of beer.

"Yep," the assured young fisherman went on, expertly feeding out line as his fish made another downstream sashay. "Yep," he repeated, nicely taking up slack on the retrieve, "that's why I gave up floating this lovely river. Nearly ten years ago, just a kid. Decided then 'twas a hell of a lot more fun fishing a hundred yards of her carefully than taking off on these all-day floating picnics."

I was silent for a while. Then: "I think you've got something there," I said, and I meant it. Of course he was right, and I was simply out joy-riding past the good fishing. I should have brought along a girl or a camera. On this beautiful river if there was no rise a float was simply an enforced if lovely scenic tour. If there was a rise, no decent fisherman ever needed to float. Presto, I now had it all figured out. . . .

"Wanna get by?" the poised young fisherman said, flipping his cigarette into the water.

"I'll wait," I said. "I got all day. My pal isn't meeting me till dark—'way down at the old burned logging bridge."

"Hm . . . trust you brought your passport—you really are out on a voyage," he said. "Perhaps you'd better slip by, fella—by the feel of this customer it'll be at least ten-twenty minutes more. Like a smart woman in the mood for play, these big trout don't like to be rushed. C'mon, just bear in sort of close to me, over here, right under London Bridge. It won't bother us at all."

My easy young philosopher evidently didn't want me to see how really big his fish was. But being a fisherman myself I knew, I knew. "All right," I said, lifting the anchor and sculling down over his way and under his throbbing line. "Thanks and good luck."

"Thanks, chum," he said, grinning at me. "Have a nice ride and good luck to you."

"Looks like I'll need it," I said, looking enviously back

over my shoulder at his trembling rod tip. "Hey," I said, belatedly remembering my company manners, "want a nice warm can of beer?"

Smiling: "Despite your glowing testimonial, no thanks."

"You're welcome," I said, realizing we were carrying on like a pair of strange diplomats.

"And one more thing, please," he said, raising his voice a little to be heard over the burbling water, still smiling intently at his straining fish. "If you don't mind, please keep this little stretch under your hat—it's been all mine for nearly ten years. It's really something special. No use kidding you —I see you've spotted my bulging creel and I guess by now you've got a fair idea of what I'm on to. And anyway I've got to take a little trip. But I'll be back—soon I hope. In the meantime try to be good to the place. I know it will be good to you."

"Right!" I shouted, for by then I had floated nearly around the downstream bend. "Mum's the word." He waved his free hand and then was blotted from view by a tall doomed spruce leaning far down out across the river from a crumbling water-blasted bank. The last thing I saw was the gleaming flash of his rod, the long taut line, the strumming leader. It made a picture I've never forgotten.

That was the last time ever that I floated the Big Escanaba River. I had learned my lesson well. Always after that when I visited this fabled new spot I hiked in, packing my gear, threading my way down river through a pungent needled maze of ancient deer trails, like a fleeing felon keeping always slyly away from the broad winding river itself. My strategy was twofold: to prevent other sly fishermen from finding and deflowering the place, and to save myself an extra mile of walking.

Despite the grand fishing I discovered there, I did not go back too often. It was a place to hoard and save, being indeed most good to me, as advertised. And always I fished it alone, for a fisherman's pact had been made, a pact that became increasingly hard to keep as the weeks rolled into months, the seasons into years, during which I never again encountered my poised young fisherman. In the morbid pathology of trout fishermen such a phenomenon is mightily disturbing. What had become of my fisherman? Hadn't he ever got back from his trip? Was he sick or had he moved away? Worse yet, had he died? How could such a consummate young artist have possibly given up fishing such an enchanted spot? Was he one of that entirely mad race of eccentric fishermen who cannot abide the thought of sharing a place, however fabulous, with even *one* other fisherman?

By and by, with the innocent selfishness possessed by all fishermen, I dwelt less and less upon the probable fate of my young fisherman and instead came smugly to think it was I who had craftily discovered the place. Nearly twenty fishing seasons slipped by on golden wings, as fishing seasons do, during which time I, fast getting no sprightlier, at last found it expedient to locate and hack out a series of abandoned old logging roads to let me drive within easier walking distance of my secret spot. The low cunning of middle age was replacing the hot stamina of youth. . . . As a road my new trail was strictly a spring-breaking bronco-buster, but at least I was able to sit and ride, after a fashion, thus saving my aging legs for the real labor of love to follow.

Another fishing season was nearly done when, one afternoon, brooding over that gloomy fact, I suddenly tore off my lawyer-mask and fled my office, heading for the Big Escanaba, bouncing and bucking my way in, finally hitting the

Glide—as I had come to call the place—about sundown. For a long time I just stood there on the high bank, drinking in the sights and pungent river smells. No fish were rising, and slowly, lovingly, I went through the familiar ritual of rigging up: scrubbing out a fine new leader, dressing the tapered line, jointing the rod and threading the line, pulling on the tall patched waders, anointing myself with fly dope. No woman dressing for a ball was more fussy. . . . Then I composed myself on my favorite fallen log and waited. I smoked a slow pipe and sipped a can of beer, cold this time, thanks to the marvels of dry ice and my new road. My watching spot overlooked a wide bend and commanded a grand double view: above, the deep slow velvet glide with its little feeder stream where I first met my young fisherman; below a sporty and productive broken run of white water stretching nearly a half-mile. The old leaning spruce that used to be there below me had long since bowed in surrender and been swept away by some forgotten spring torrent. As I sat waiting the wind had died, the shadowing waters had taken on the brooding blue hush of evening, the dying embers of sundown suddenly lit a great blazing forest fire in the tops of the tall spruces across river from me, and an unknown bird that I have always called simply the "lonely" bird sang timidly its ancient haunting plaintive song. I arose and took a deep breath like a soldier advancing upon the enemy.

The fisherman's mystic hour was at hand.

First I heard and then saw a young buck in late velvet slowly, tentatively splashing his way across to my side, above me and beyond the feeder creek, ears twitching and tall tail nervously wigwagging. Then he winded me, freezing in midstream, giving me a still and liquid stare for a poised instant; then came charging on across in great pawing incredibly graceful leaps, lacquered flanks quivering, white flag up and waving, bounding up the bank and into the anonymous woods, the sounds of his excited blowing fading and growing fainter and then dying away.

In the meantime four fair trout had begun rising in the smooth tail of the glide just below me. I selected and tied on a favorite small dry fly and got down below the lowest riser and managed to take him on the first cast, a short dainty float. Without moving I stood and lengthened line and took all four risers, all nice firm brook trout upwards of a foot, all the time purring and smirking with increasing complacency. The omens were good. As I relit my pipe and waited for new worlds to conquer I heard a mighty splash above me and wheeled gaping at the spreading magic ring of a really good trout, carefully marking the spot. Oddly enough he had risen just above where the young buck had just crossed, a little above the feeder creek. Perhaps, I thought extravagantly, perhaps he was after the deer. . . . I waited, tense and watchful, but he did not rise again.

I left the river and scrambled up the steep gravelly bank and made my way through the tall dense spruces up to the little feeder creek. I slipped down the bank like a footpad, stealthily inching my way out to the river in the silted creek itself, so as not to scare the big one, *my* big one. I could feel the familiar shock of icy cold water suddenly clutching at my ankles as I stood waiting at the spot where I had first run across my lost fisherman. I quickly changed to a fresh fly in the same pattern, carefully snubbing the knot. Then the fish obediently rose again, a savage easy engulfing roll, again the undulant outgoing ring, just where I had marked him, not more than thirty feet from me and a little beyond the middle and obliquely upstream. Here was, I saw, a cagey selective riser, lord of his pool, and one who would not suffer fools gladly. So I commanded myself to rest him before casting. "Twenty-one, twenty-two, twenty-three . . ." I counted.

The cast itself was indecently easy and, finally releasing it, the little Adams sped out on its quest, hung poised in mid-air for an instant, and then settled sleepily upon the water like a thistle, uncurling before the leader like the languid outward folding of a ballerina's arm. The fly circled a moment, uncertainly, then was caught by the current. Down, down it rode, closer, closer, then—*clap!*—the fish rose and kissed it, I flicked my wrist and he was on, and then away he went roaring off downstream, past feeder creek and happy fisherman, the latter hot after him.

During the next mad half-hour I fought this explosive creature up and down the broad stream, up and down, ranging at least a hundred feet each way, or so it seemed, without ever once seeing him. This meant, I figured, that he was either a big brown or a brook. A rainbow would surely have leapt a dozen times by now. Finally I worked him into the deep safe water off the feeder creek where he sulked nicely while I panted and rested my benumbed rod arm. As twilight receded into dusk with no sign of his tiring I began vaguely to wonder just who had latched on to whom. For the fifth or sixth time I rested my aching arm by transferring the rod to my left hand, professionally shaking out my tired wrist just as I had once seen a young fisherman do.

Nonchalantly I reached in my jacket and got out and tried to light one of my rigidly abominable Italian cigars. My fish, unimpressed by my show of aplomb, shot suddenly away on a powerful zigzag exploratory tour upstream, the fisherman nearly swallowing his unlit cigar as he scrambled up after him. It was then that I saw a lone man sitting quietly in a canoe, anchored in midstream above me. The tip of his fly rod showed over the stern. My heart sank:

after all these years my hallowed spot was at last discovered.

"Hi," I said, trying to convert a grimace of pain into an amiable grin, all the while keeping my eye on my sulking fish. The show must go on.

"Hi," he said.

"How you doin'?" I said, trying to make a brave show of casual fish talk.

"Fairish," he said, "but nothing like you seem to be on to."

"Oh, he isn't so much," I said, lying automatically if not too well. "I'm working a fine leader and don't dare to bull him." At least that was the truth.

The stranger laughed briefly and glanced at his wrist watch. "You've been on to him that I know of for over forty minutes—and I didn't see you make the strike. Let's not try to kid the Marines. I just moved down a bit closer to be in on the finish. I'll shove away if you think I'm too close."

"Nope," I answered generously, delicately snubbing my fish away from a partly submerged windfall. "But about floating this lovely river," I pontificated, "there's nothing in it, my friend. Absolutely nothing. Gave it up myself eighteen-twenty years ago. Figured out it was better working one stretch carefully than shoving off on these floating picnics. Recommend it to you, comrade."

The man in the canoe was silent. I could see the little red moon of his cigarette glowing and fading in the gathering gloom. Perhaps my gratuitous pedagogical ruminations had offended him; after all, trout fishermen are a queer proud race. Perhaps I should try diversionary tactics. "Wanna get by?" I inquired silkily. Maybe I could get him to go away before I tried landing this unwilling porpoise. He still remained silent. "Wanna get by?" I repeated. "It's perfectly O.K. by me. As you see—it's a big roomy river."

"No," he said dryly. "No thanks." There was another long

pause. Then: "If you wouldn't mind too much I think I'll put in here for the night. It's getting pretty late—and somehow I've come to like the looks of this spot."

"Oh," I said in a small voice—just "Oh"—as I disconsolately watched him lift his anchor and expertly push his canoe in to the near gravelly shore, above me, where it grated halfway in and scraped to rest. He sat there quietly, his little neon cigarette moon glowing, and I felt I just had to say something more. After all I didn't *own* the river. "Why sure, of course, it's a beautiful place to camp, plenty of pine knots for fuel, a spring-fed creek for drinking water and cooling your beer," I ran on gaily, rattling away like an hysterical realtor trying to sell the place. Then I began wondering how I would ever spirit my noisy fish car out of the woods without the whole greedy world of fishermen learning about my new secret road to this old secret spot. Maybe I'd even have to abandon it for the night and hike out. . . . Then I remembered there was an unco-operative fish to be landed, so I turned my full attention to the unfinished and uncertain business at hand. "Make yourself at home," I lied softly.

"Thanks," the voice again answered dryly, and again I heard the soft chuckle in the semidarkness.

My fish had stopped his mad rushes now and was busily boring the bottom, the long leader vibrating like the plucked string of a harp. For the first time I found I was able gently to pump him up for a cautious look. And again I almost swallowed my still unlit stump of cigar as I beheld his dorsal fin cleaving the water nearly a foot back from the fly. He wallowed and shook like a dog and then rolled on his side, then recovered and fought his way back down and away on another run, but shorter this time. With a little pang I knew then that my fish was a done, but the pang quickly passed—it always did—and again I gently, relentlessly pumped him up, shortening line, drawing him in to the familiar daisy hoop of landing range, kneeling and stretching and straining out my opposing aching arms like those of an extravagant archer. The net slipped fairly under him on the first try and, clenching my cigar, I made my pass and lo! lifted him free and dripping from the water. "Ah-h-h . . ." He was a glowing superb spaniel-sized brown. I staggered drunkenly away from the water and sank anywhere to the ground, panting like a winded miler.

"Beautiful, *beautiful*," I heard my forgotten and unwelcome visitor saying like a prayer. "I've dreamed all this— over a thousand times I've dreamed it."

I tore my feasting eyes away from my fish and glowered up at the intruder. He was half standing in the beached canoe now, one hand on the side, trying vainly to wrest the cap from a bottle, of all things, seeming in the dusk to smile uncertainly. I felt a sudden chill sense of concern, of vague nameless alarm.

"Look, chum," I said, speaking lightly, very casually, "is everything all O.K.?"

"Yes, yes, of course," he said shortly, still plucking away at his bottle. "There . . . I—I'm coming now."

Bottle in hand he stood up and took a resolute broad step out of the canoe, then suddenly, clumsily he lurched and pitched forward, falling heavily, cruelly, half in the beached canoe and half out upon the rocky wet shore. For a moment I sat staring ruefully, then I scrambled up and started running toward him, still holding my rod and the netted fish, thinking this fisherman was indubitably potted. "No, no, no!" he shouted at me, struggling and scrambling to his feet in a kind of wild urgent frenzy. I halted, frozen, holding my sagging dead fish as the intruder limped toward me, in a curious sort of creaking stiffly mechanical limp, the uncorked but still intact bottle held triumphantly aloft in one muddy wet hand, the other hand reaching gladly toward me.

"Guess I'll never get properly used to this particular battle stripe," he said, slapping his thudding and unyielding right leg. "But how are you, stranger?" he went on, his wet eyes glistening, his bruised face smiling. "How about our having a drink to your glorious trout—and still another to reunion at our old secret fishing spot?"

14

These Tired Old Eyes . . .

THESE tired old eyes have beheld some fairly strange sights during the years they have guided this fisherman on his trout devotionals. Sometimes I suspect that fishermen while practicing their favorite vice are peculiarly well situated to observe nature with her hair down. Perhaps it is the very intentness and detachment of fishermen during their seizures. Perhaps their obliviousness to all but the business at hand somehow communicates itself to the rest of the forest and water dwellers so that they in turn are lulled into going about their normal pursuits with a calm they would rarely possess under the conscious search and scrutiny of the hunters or professional bird and animal watchers. At any rate fishermen are at least suffered if not accepted by the wild things of nature; and if they, the fishermen, would but look away more often from their fishing they would doubtless observe even stranger sights than they do. Here are some droll sights and experiences, just a few, that I have run across in my addled wanderings after trout.

On several occasions I have come upon a mother porcupine prone on her back nursing her young, a unique position which I have heard that the females of these prickly animals likewise maintain while begetting them—though my quill is somewhat uncertain on this latter point.

While on a fishing trip that I have mentioned elsewhere I have seen a skunk swim leisurely across a broad river, its tail arched proudly so as to keep its powder dry. I have also come upon rabbits and groundhogs nestling up in trees, an arboreal environment not normally associated with these creatures.

I have watched a pair of otter slip up over a beaver dam and assault and boldly gut the place of its trout while I stood there unarmed and helpless, trying vainly to drive them away with the few rocks I could find. It was a blitzkrieg and a harrowing spectacle to watch. One undulant otter patrolled the upstream escape outlet, flashing back and forth at incredible speed, while the other robber did the real dirty work, both chomping their jaws horribly each time they came up for air. Creation of panic and their lightning speed seemed to be their chief weapons. It was then that I learned thoroughly to loathe otter; so much so that I refuse to succumb to the obvious pun that there otter be a law against otter. If they would *only* confine their depredations to bass I'd start breeding them . . .

This was the same strange season that I swear I caught more birds and insects and assorted reptiles and flying things than trout. A typical entry follows:

"Caught a dragonfly on a 16 Trude on my back cast out at Frenchman's Pond. Kept pumping away at the forward cast and nothing happened, a creepy feeling. Looked back and there was the dragonfly, himself pumping away like mad, trying vainly to drag my fly and flyline in the opposite direction. Put down rod, donned my rubber gloves, and performed minor surgery before order was restored. Dr. T. Wellington Cole scrubbed with me. Suspect this may be as much evidence of the nearsightedness of dragonflies as a tribute to the expertness of my fly-tier."

This same thing happened *three* times that same season; though it never happened before and hasn't since. That enchanted summer I also caught two bats and two unknown birds on my back casts, a swooping swallow-like bird on my forward cast, and three frogs, a fish duck, a snapping turtle and two garter snakes in the water. Toward the end of that season I find this wistful entry: "Must remember to start a zoo. It'll have everything but fish!"

On another expedition Gunnar Anderson, Tom Bennett, and Gipp Warner and I boated up the Big Dead basin. All of us were hilarious and feeling no pain. We put in at the eerily squawking heron rookery near the mouth of Wahlman's Creek to try for the big brook trout that sometimes lurk there. Long time nothing. Then I finally snubbed on to a fair trout on a sunken hair fly. Gunnar netted him and dressed him out and cast the entrails overboard, chortling, "This will bring the big ones around." Then he reached over to rinse off the trout. The trout slipped out of his hand—*pop* —and *swam* gracefully and deliberately down out of sight! We looked at each other wide-eyed and soberly weighed anchor and got the hell out of there. I know a little something about the possibility of muscular spasms, instinctive reactions, and habit responses and all that, but don't *ever* let it happen to you!

Here is another odd one for the book:

"At 5:30 this morning took a nice 13-inch brook at the

high sand-bank-bend on the East Branch. Number 12 Mc-Ginty, dry. Had court that day so reluctantly quit at seven. Cleaned out my trout at gravel ford by washed-out bridge. Found partly digested bait hook in gut of largest trout. Met Gipp in town that morning and, since he and I fish that stretch a lot, started to tell him about finding hook. He stopped me and said: 'You caught the fish at the high sand bank, didn't you? He was over twelve inches. The hook was an eagle claw, about number 8, snelled, with red wrappings, with about two inches of leader left above the shank?' He paused. 'My wife lost that fish at 9:30 last night.' "

It was the same fish, of course, but the point is that a trout started feeding again within such a few hours after such a harrowing experience (contrary to many fish dopesters) and further, that during that short time he had nearly digested a hook that would loom relatively the size of a whale harpoon in our own bellies. Small wonder that the more one fishes for trout the less he pretends to know about them.

Here is an entry from my fish notes:

"My old fishing pal, Louie Bonetti, took me on another of his celebrated goose chases, this time down the Fifteen Hill Creek. 'Are you *sure* I can fly fish down there, Louie?' I cross-examined him carefully before we started, still smarting over past wild-goose expeditions led by the dauntless and irrepressible Louie. 'Sure, sure t'ing, Yon,' Louie grinned, 'you can fly lak ever't'ing!' He was right. We hadn't proceeded a hundred yards through this jungle before I realized wryly that the only way to properly present a fly in that creek was to fly over and drop it from a balloon. I could hear Louie ahead of me, threshing along like a bull elephant in must, pausing here and there to drop his bait into the murky waters. It was like trying to fish in a green barrel. After ruining one leader and losing three flies I shrugged philosophically and folded my rod and creeled my net and bowed my head in defeat. I longed only to get out of there. I had been taken again. . . .

" 'Yon!' Louie shouted. 'Luke at dis! Come queeck, luke at dis!' I finally crashed into a clearing big enough to accommodate a telephone booth, and there was Louie proudly holding a ten-inch brook trout he had just taken on a big nightcrawler. From the mouth of the still-wriggling trout protruded four inches of another trout's tail! As I watched, Louie pulled on the tail and extracted what was left of a seven-inch trout! A cannibalistic ten-inch trout had eaten— or was eating—a seven-inch trout, and still had found the greedy appetite and room to cram Louie's porkchop bait on top of that! 'W'at you tink?' Louie asked me. 'Me, I think it's time for a drink,' I said, reaching in Louie's knapsack for his trusty pint bottle."

Another day Louie Bonetti and I were boating up a remote stretch of the Middle Escanaba, when hawk-eyed Louie spotted a little spotted fawn lying amongst the water-worn rocks that lined the exposed shore line below a high tangled bank. We assumed that it and its mother had come down for a drink or for respite from flies, so we went merrily on our way, the discovered fawn watching us out of sight with its soft liquid eyes. Many hours later, floating back down in the dusk, we saw that the fawn was still there. I was about to shrug and float on but Louie insisted that we put in. "Non, non, we stop. Somet'ing goddam a wrong a dis place, Yon," he said.

There was. As we approached the shore the fawn stood up on its spindly, wavering legs and bleated in terror, at the same time pulling out to the end of a chain which anchored a large double-spring trap, the rusty jaws of which we discovered were clamped tightly across the right foreleg just above the exquisite tiny hoof. I held the trembling creature from plunging while Louie tenderly released the jaws of the trap. We then carried the bleating fawn up the high bank and set it upon level ground. It continued to bleat and cry piteously. "Ma-a-ma!" it called. "Whew," answered the unseen mother from deep in the woods. *"Whew, whew!"* we could hear her thudding back and forth in the thick cover, running in quick thumping nervous trots.

The fawn took a few tentative limping steps in the direction of the woods and then *ran* on all *four* legs to join its mother, bleating gaily. Louie and I grinned and nodded and resumed our twilit float down the misty Escanaba, both of us swollen with virtue over the good turn we had done an otherwise doomed fawn.

"Damma dose coyote trappers," Louie swore darkly. "Why dey leave a dose set trap lay 'round for poor little fella catcha his foot in?" *This* burst of sentiment was from a man who had shot more deer than most men have ever seen. . . .

On still another day Louie and I were fishing a rather tangled but productive brook up near Silver Lake. When we met back at the car at dusk, a puffing and breathless Louie announced he had just met a "beeg" black bear on the trail. Louie, who always acted out everything that ever happened to him, crouched down on all fours.

"I coma down trail an' ducka my head under t'ick bush lak a dis—an' w'en I stan' up dere's dis beeg blacka bear stan' right dere on front of me—so close I can see even his little red eyes lak peeg, an' smell his bad breat'."

"What'd you do, Louie?" I said, wondering how the lucky bear ever got away from Louie.

"Hm . . . Wan time I hear some place, I dunno, some people he say if man say somet'ing to wile animal he liable get scare an' run lak a hell."

"Yes?" I prompted.

"Well, dis a here beeg black bear he stan' dere an' luke at me an' I stan' dere luke at him—so den I queeck remember w'at I hear. 'Say somet'ing, Louie!' I t'ink. So I tip my hat lak dis, real polite, an' smile real nice an' I say reala loud, 'Gooda mornin', Mister Bear!' "

"What'd the bear do?"

"Hm . . . he get scare lak da people say an' run lak a hell nudder way."

"What'd you do, Louie?"

"Hm . . . Louie he *stay* awful scare an' run lak a hell dis a way. . . . Boy oh boy, le's have da beeg drink!"

To attempt to do justice to this rare man Louie would require a five-foot shelf of books. *Everything* happened to Louie—including the final awful day two autumns ago when the bullet from an old friend's deer rifle unerringly found its way into Louie's belly. Louie had been mistaken for a deer. He died the next morning and the whole county went into mourning. But the saga of Louie Bonetti will cling to his name for many years. I can only faintly suggest the pungent flavor of the man here.

Perhaps the most moving woods spectacle I have ever seen while fishing happened several years ago and the record of which I quote from my fishing notes:

"Yesterday on Loon Lake I saw the unfolding of a thrilling and saddening forest tragedy. I was prowling the north side of the lake when suddenly I heard a great commotion and squawking from the southwest corner, nearly a half-mile away. Looking I saw a wild duck and a great loon engaged in battle. It was a case of David versus Goliath, the little duck seeming to be the aggressor. I quickly put my binoculars on them. I cannot describe the fierceness of the combat;

the incredible darting swiftness of it. At length the duck retreated, the loon following, the duck skeetering just over the top of the water as though wounded, always *just* out of reach of the pursuing loon. Then the truth dawned on me: this was a mother duck doubtless protecting her young and putting on the ancient lame-duck act. At any rate, the loon suddenly submarined and the duck, at the real risk of her life, still kept skeetering, flapping the very surface of the water, luring the loon on and away from her young, whose terrified cheeping now came thinly across the water. I never did see the young ducks. At length the mother duck rose in flight, and almost immediately the great loon popped out of the water where the duck had just been. The duck circled in low flight back to her young. She banked and skidded into a little bay and the terrified cheeping ceased.

"In the meantime I had ignored my fly and it had sunk to the bottom. I flipped the line to raise it—and was on to a good trout. While I was preoccupiedly landing this fish the loon returned to the ducks, and the very same battle ensued, except that this time the loon showed signs of giving up the pursuit and returning to the young. At this the lion-hearted mother duck again made a fierce frontal attack on the loon and again enraged it into following her virtually across the lake. And once again the loon rose from the water just as the duck lifted into flight and circled back to her young. Then I felt my rod bending and remembered I was on to a fish, my first trout on flies in tantalizing Loon Lake. I landed it. It was a plump fighting thirteen-inch brook. But I had lost all zest for fishing. I just sat and helplessly watched the distant drama, longing for a rifle to plug the bullying loon. Although the loon stalked the ducks all afternoon, schnorkeling in close, it evidently lacked the heart to again mix with the brave mother duck. At sundown I quietly folded my tent and stole away. There was no rise."

A few days later I returned, this time with a high-powered rifle with a scope sight. This is my entry for that day:

"Saturday back at Loon Lake I saw and heard a *pair* of loons giggling and cackling and diving, but no sign of the ducks. I fear the worst, namely, that the loons either ganged up and killed the gallant mother duck or else chased her away (though I think not) and ate her young. Certainly the young could not very well have flown or walked away. [NOTE: Since writing this I have indeed met a mother duck and her young walking along on land.] I was tempted to shoot the loons, but I was not sure there had been a murder or that they were the murderers. Anyway I was apparently too late. And, moreover, who was I to judge their guilt or appoint myself their executioner? I did not know that loons ate flesh, besides, possibly, fish, but now I am afraid they do. . . ."

Here I lapsed into a little gratuitous philosophizing which I shall throw in for good measure.

"The constant obscure savagery of nature seems always to lurk below the apparently placid surface of things. Probably even the lice on the loon's wings battle each other, while I know that the fish swimming below dwell in a subterranean welter of cannibalism. How can men hope for peace when combat and strife, not peace and calm, seem to be the basic norms of nature? In a real sense, then, peace is an unnatural state and all the elaborate plans of men to achieve it are, in this sense, in plain perversion of nature. Alas, peaceful men may be *unnatural* men, a fairly bleak prospect in the Atomic Age."

15

Grampaw Returners

"At last the great-hearted trout lay dripping and sagging in my net, both of us gasping from the scorching battle. I looked down at him and he rolled his glistening wet eyes up at me. Then, carefully holding him so [here follows a description in vast detail of the certified way to lovingly hold trout] I tenderly removed the fly, which miraculously hung by a bare sliver of bony cartilage, and gently held the great fish upright in the water. There he lay, fanning his great fins and desperately working his gills. After a bit I gently touched his dorsal fin, just a little pat, and he moved slowly down and away and became one with the shadowy depths. 'Farewell, great fighting old fellow—farewell and good luck. . . .'"

For years I have been hearing and reading poetic dilations like this from the great-hearted giants among fishermen, and each time I get a powerful big lump in my throat. In fact these men of heroic stature fill me with awe and I am inclined to break out all over with little goose pimples of inferiority in their presence. For I envy these gallant fishermen who are forever releasing their "big ones," and who then stand around all kind of misty-eyed and choked up while Grampaw (for whom they had been campaigning relentlessly for at least three seasons) regains his composure and swims majestically away. Indeed, some of these big fish seem to have been caught and released so often they have lost their amateur standing.

Yes, I envy these fishermen their greatness of heart and nobility of spirit but I cannot copy them. I regret that on these occasions I seem possessed of the heart of a woodtick and the spirit of a gnat. My craven character fails always to respond to the lofty challenge of the situation. I guess I simply lack the magnanimity of spirit and extravagance of soul. My really big fish are few and far between and I keep them. Furthermore, I wail like a banshee whenever I lose one.

I try to comfort myself for my deficiencies by reflecting that all trout are cannibals and that the big ones are almost exclusively so; and that by removing them from our trout waters I am really doing both the fish and my fellow fishermen a good turn. But try as I might to rationalize myself into gladness, in my secret heart I *know* that I can never really *belong;* that I am still an unregenerate and greedy peasant among true trout fishermen. Alas, *I don't return my big fish!*

But there is one thing that I do do that I don't hear quite so much about. I return a whale of a lot of small *legal* trout; and, when the prospects are good that I could have filled out, I frequently leave the stream or pond with less than my legal limit. I know that this dreary ruse will never qualify me for membership in the exclusive fishing fraternity of *Grampaw*

Returners, but I try to console myself with the notion that, as undramatic and unsung a thing as it is, and one not nearly so inflating to the fisherman's ego, it is perhaps a more sensible working fishing philosophy and one that really helps the fish and my fellow peasants.

16

Spots Before the Eyes

FISHERMEN are a cultured and worldly lot; their broad and diversified interests make them delightful and even absorbing companions; they'll talk about anything under the sun so long as it concerns fishing—preferably with themselves in a stellar role. They take a trout's-eye view of the world and see everything darkly through their own wavering, distorted, astigmatic lens of broken beer bottles. Spots and speckles dance constantly before their eyes. When they aren't fishing they gabble and prattle about fishing much as clusters of idle women run on about babies and clothes—and the witch-like tendencies of *other* women. So it is that the following grab bag of trout prejudice and gossip concerns itself not so much with actual fishing as with the trivia of fishing, like the chatter of earnest boy scouts who temporarily forsake the solemn business of tying bowlines and rubbing dry sticks together, to sit around the campfire and compare the various wrenches and reamers and other burglar tools that adorn their respective scout knives. On with the small talk.

Outdoor Fish Fries: The flesh of the trout is a rare delicacy that comes from one of nature's most tender and perishable creatures. Trout were never designed to be embalmed along with the steaks and ox joints of the aristocracy of the new Ice Age in their well-larded deep freezers. Trout should be eaten not later than twenty-four hours after they are caught, else one might better eat damp swamp hay crowned with chain-store mayonnaise. But by far the best time to enjoy your trout is beside the waters where they are caught. Take a fry pan along and some bacon or shortening, and a little cornmeal and salt, and have yourself a feast fit for a deposed king—or an ulcerated millionaire. But first take a trout. . . .

Competition in Fishing: A trout stream is a poor place for gambling and much of the reflective charm of fishing is lost by making a surly competition out of the undertaking. I will have no part of a fishing party made up of those fishing prima donnas whose very manhood seems to depend on being top rod. Yet my regular trout pals and I have worked out a standing wager on our fishing, and far from making us surly it is surprising how much added zest and friendly fun this adds to our sport. Anyone that does get surly about it is fired out of the lodge. This is our bet: we each pay the winner a dollar for the longest trout over twelve inches. The loser's ante jumps to two bucks a head if the longest fish goes fifteen inches or over.

The net result of this is good; we find ourselves more and more frequently returning a lot of legal-sized trout we might otherwise have kept; and when we meet and decide to quit "in just five minutes more" there is always the delicious uncertainty and the long chance that the Mister Tanglefoot of the day will make one last desperate cast and—*whambo!*—walk away with the honors. It has happened. Frequently, of course, no fish qualify, but there have been times when three or more of us have had to get out our calipers and crouch to see just who had won the two-dollar bet. These occasions have usually involved lunking browns or rainbows, but it has also happened with brooks.

Trout Sense: There is no substitute for fishing sense, and if a man doesn't have it, verily, he may cast like an angel and still use his creel largely to transport sandwiches and beer. I have friends whom I can mechanically outfish in practically every department of the sport yet who in their comparatively crude way still manage to tie into any big trout that happen to be lying about. They also continue regularly to relieve me of my wrinkled dollar bills. Then again I have fishing friends—several of them holders of enviable casting records—who can in turn outfish me in nearly every department but who sometimes even more sadly than I seem to lack that indescribable sixth sense that guides the flies of some fishermen into the very jaws of lurking "soakers."

Without growing mystic over this, some men seem to "think like a fish" more than others. They are the smart ones who can take one look at a pool or a riffle and sense immediately where to pause and plop their sloppy, ill-delivered casts, when all the while we Fancy Dans are posturing grandly over here or over there, unerringly sending out long whistling dramatic casts over the favorite lies of old tomato cans.

Once in a blue moon a fisherman comes along who combines this mysterious fish sense with superb casting ability and all the rest. I have known one or two of these diabolical fellows. He is the magician we other fishermen should take up collections for in order to persuade *him* to take up golf. There is no other way to keep the trout away from him. He can catch fish in a rain barrel. My current fishing pal, Henry Scarffe, is fast moving into this class. Some men are said to have sex appeal; *these* characters possess trout appeal, and I swear that many a happily married lady trout will forsake even her snug spawning bed to succumb to his lure. He is also the suave one who makes all the rest of us pedestrian fishermen look like slipping and fumbling political hacks out taking creel census in borrowed waders.

Glass Rods: I am now reluctantly satisfied that glass fly rods are mechanically the equal of and perhaps often perform better than the best bamboo rods. Not only that, they are more reasonable in price; require little or no care; and apparently last forever. I'll concede all that, but never will I let another glass fly rod darken my door. Put it down, if you will, to a burst of girlish sentiment of the heart or middle-aged sediment on the kidneys—I'll take split bamboo. To my mind there is no fairy wand in creation more graceful and beautiful than a good bamboo fly rod. They *look* so good; they *feel* so good. Like fingerprints, no two bamboo rods are alike; each is an individual possessed of its own unique character and one that a fisherman can really get to know.

But these gleaming impersonal glass rods that some chemist has conceived in a laboratory out of skimmed milk and old box tops, these synthetic concoctions that are turned out on an assembly line as much alike as two peas in a pod, simply aren't for me. I'd sooner cast over glass *fish* than use one. I love my bamboo fly rods and I choose to think they have a sneaking yen for me. But I'm afraid I can never quite fall in love with a chemist's incestuous brain child. In short 'tis a pox I wish on all glass rods. (Adv.: I'll sell you a dandy for five bucks.)

Creels: Conventional bulging wicker creels are handy to carry beer in, and they also look nice and woodsy when freshly varnished and hanging from the wall of a den. Aside from that they are clumsy, brush-snagging, foul-smelling nuisances. Get yourself a *flat*, loose-meshed matting creel, one that will nicely accommodate your landing net for travel or brushy going. If you *must* remain a slave to synthetics, then get a flat plastic one, damn it. Either variety is easily washable and thus does not attract the sea gulls and blow-flies for miles around.

Simple Refrigeration: One of those tightly covered round popcorn tins the kids keep trundling home together with some of those little cans of solution you pre-freeze solid in your icebox (and use over and over) make a non-messy and fine combination for cooling beer and keeping perishables. They are also nice to preserve that big trout you bought from Julius the guide to prove to your wife you were not out wading with squaws or dallying with blondes.

Guides on Fly Rods: They're way too small and they should be made of chromium or some other bland non-abrasive metal. I believe as many fly lines are ruined by the constant sawing and rasping through these niggardly conventional fine-wire snake guides as are ruined by the twin plagues of mildew and improper storage. Since there are from nine to thirteen of these wizened hacksaw guides on the average fly rod, I sometimes suspect that the line and rod people must have conspired to continue using them. I have a seven-foot glass combination spinning and fly rod, and when fly fishing with it—I rarely do—I use a lovely torpedoed-in-series Marvin Hedge silk fly line. In places where I can get a decent backcast verily I believe I can paste out nearly as much line in a controlled cast as I can with my best bamboo fly rod. Part of this is due to the rippled torpedo feature, no doubt, but a good part I believe is due to the larger, smoother, free-running spinning guides. At any rate I can really shoot the cast. Next winter I'm going to try an experiment and have a set of spinning guides put on one of my bamboo fly rods. Perhaps I'll still shame these unimaginative and smug medieval fly-rod makers into following suit.

On Getting Lost: If you are really lost and it is dusk, build a rough camp and compose yourself until the thundering horde comes to find you. Most people seem to display a morbid sort of missionary zeal in finding lost brethren. Conserve your matches for smoke signals. If it is still daylight follow a trout stream, if you are on or near one, and you should soon come to a broad trail beaten by the army of faithful fishermen. More lost men come to grief from panic and exhaustion than anything else. Remember, when you are lost you are only temporarily in a state that was permanent to your hardy ancestors. Keep your chin up and your temperature down, and above all use your head before your legs.

An obvious clue overlooked by many confused fishermen is secondary roads and trails. If a road or trail you are following forks off into two or more roads or trails, you may safely conclude that you are going the wrong way and that "civilization" lies the other way. All roads and trails fork off *away* from home plate. Simply follow the point of the V. Think it over. . . . Again, if you see car tracks on a road with water puddles you can easily tell the direction the car has gone by the tire marks. The tracks are visible entering the puddle but become obliterated by the splashing cargo of water as they leave. Follow the car. If it has gone to camp it shouldn't be far; if it has gone to town, that's for you, too. And if, while following the tracks, you come to a fork, you can also thus confirm which way the car was heading, town or woodsward.

Leaders: Leaders are the problem child of fishing; they are far and away the weakest weapon in the fisherman's arsenal. All leaders are necessarily an uneasy compromise between the fisherman's normal desire to hold a decent fish if he gets on to one and his awareness that it is neither sporting nor productive of rises to employ a logging chain. Theoretically a leader should be invisible, and the only way to approach this diabolic goal is to keep using finer leaders. The main drawback with this strategy, however, is that the finer the leader the less liable it is to survive the initial shock of the strike; yet, *once a fish is on,* it is surprising how much strain even the finest leader can stand.

I have found a simple way to lessen this frequently fatal initial impact on fine leaders and, good fellow that I am, I pass it on to you. It is especially good on still clear waters where one must employ hair-thin leaders. It is this: Simply affix a common rubber elastic band between the end of your fly line and the butt end of your leader. It's the neatest little shock-absorber on the market. Think it over—and then go forth and try it.

Not only does this stratagem help with the initial shock but it also helps greatly to reduce the danger of loss in play during those thrilling moments when you discover that your fish is heavier than you bargained for and it is touch and go whether you can hold on to him at all.

Slow Intermittent Rises: For good fishing give me these any time over the boiling and dramatic general rise. The latter is apt to be highly selective, and especially so on still waters. When trout are choosy every fly in the kit is apt to be the wrong one or else the right one is spurned if it is not presented and handled in precisely the right way. On the other hand a fairly steady but intermittent riser usually represents a fish gnawed by hunger and one more likely to snaffle any interesting morsel that drifts within its ken. Another thing, an occasional riser seems to range farther from his lie for food than does a rapid feeder on a particular fly hatch; hence the fisherman's cast need not be so delicately exact.

I remember a pair of such slow risers one evening at dusk on a deep, narrow run on the East Branch of the Escanaba. They were rising so seldom I almost passed them by. At first I tried approaching them from below but could not get within decent casting range because of brush and deep water. The approach from upstream was better but since they lay at the loop of a sharp double curve, the difficult slack-line downstream dry-fly float was not feasible. It looked as if I would practically have to go pat them on the nose to decently present a fly.

I did just that. I appproached them warily from above, the only way I could, inching along with infinite caution. When one would rise I'd move another foot closer. Finally they stayed down so long I thought I had put them down for good. Then both rose simultaneously. So, with scarcely more line out than twice the length of my rod, I dapped, not floated, a dry fly above the top riser. He immediately rose and nailed it. I powered him away from his cousin and fought him to net with only the leader showing. Without moving I tried the same strategy with the second riser—and also tied into him on the first try. They were a nice pair of fighting brook trout, but I perhaps wouldn't have had a Chinaman's chance to take either of them if they hadn't been hungry, less careful, and quite nonselective in their diet.

Another time I maneuvered for hours, it seemed, to get in casting position below a big intermittent riser on the Middle Branch. His lie was one of the many fisherman's headaches —inshore and directly under some low-lying tag alder branches—but I still saw a faint chance to float in a morsel over him. It was a delicate situation; one sloppy cast or false move would surely drive him down. In my mind's eye I could see him lying there just above me, fanning away and avidly watching everything, owly with hunger.

I concluded I had to do it on the first try or fail; it was all or nothing. So I made my false casts, back and forth, back and forth, measuring and calculating like a perspiring diamond cutter about to split a fabulous gem. Then, just as I released the business cast, the fly ticked a protruding tag alder twig and dropped like a sash weight, striking the water —spat—about four feet below my fish. Before I could let out an anguished yelp—or do anything else—that fish literally turned a somersault around and lunged downstream, nailing the fly. All hell couldn't have gotten it away from him! After a thrilling tussle amidst the awful tangle of half-submerged tag alder boughs I finally brought him to net. He was a monster brown with a yawning cannibalistic head like a tarpon. Part of his tail still stuck up out of the net, he was that big. And I didn't put him back. But the point is that I no more deserved to catch that fish than, I feel, I deserved to fail to catch so many others I have stalked and presented the fly to perfectly—only to have them spurn my most adroit and gorgeous offerings.

One-Man Boats: Most so-called one-man boats designed for trout fishing on inland waters could be better employed in harpooning whales off the storm-lashed coast of Newfoundland. These craft are usually far too big and heavy. Indeed, the average man would be hard put to trundle their *oars* any distance. And their designers evidently think that fly-fishermen mount and employ a windlass to crank in their trout; at least they build their monstrosities accordingly. In fact these builders possess a positive low genius for not knowing what in hell they're doing. The requirements for a one-man trout boat are few and simple: it should be small, light, safe, silent, and easily portable. But try and find one.

There are some new light metal one- and two-man boats seeping into the market that are in all respects the candy rig except for two bad features—they cost nearly their weight in gold and, worse yet, they make too damn much noise. Either the fisherman is forever accidentally banging the thing with his paddle or the varying water pressures are bulging and buckling the metal hide. *"Clank, clunk!"* I have a spendthrift friend, proud fellow, who possesses a new one, and a gleaming thing it is. The only trouble is that his clanging progress along a trout stream or pond sounds not unlike that rural legal giant, Justice of the Peace Paulson, whanging away at his tall brass cuspidor. Remember? All the terrified trout for miles around promptly go down and stay down. Now when we two go a-boating for trout I usually spend half my time getting to hell away from him.

I have three fishing boats: a light canvas-covered duck boat that I occasionally use on placid trout ponds; then a sturdy nine-foot cedar boat that I use on rougher ponds and

lakes and rocky rivers and also when I use my fishtail pro-
peller; and then an eight-foot rubber boat with twin in-
flatable bladders, sort of like pregnant hot dogs laid end to
end. This last is my pet and is the best all-around one-man
trout boat I have ever seen. (Isn't it nice that I like my
equipment?) It is light, safe and silent; I can easily carry it
and my fishing gear a quarter or half mile, inflated, if the
going isn't too thick; and if it is I can deflate and pack it in
and then inflate it with a hand pump or air cartridge. It is
tough (I bought it way before the War) and has never once
snagged or punctured.

I always prefer to wade when wading is feasible but so
much of our glaciated country possesses such suicidally
unwadable waters that I think my best fishing waters would
be reduced by at least half if it weren't for my faithful old
rubber boat. I have waded certain stretches of our rivers
right up the middle and been only ankle deep, while only
a few yards away yawned deep watery craters large enough
to engulf a cathedral, pigeon guano and all, and leave not a
trace. In fact I suspect some of them do harbor sunken
cathedrals because on quiet evenings I sometimes seem to
hear the stifled pealing of far-off watery bells. . . . At any
rate, these hidden river caverns may be nice hiding places
for big fish but they're rather wearing on the nerve ends of
big wading fishermen.

The only trouble with my rubber boat is that it is getting
pretty battered and old and leaky—like its skipper—and the
first money I get ahead I'm going to send and get me an
exact duplicate. It's strictly a honey and when this book is
hatched and flutters soundlessly upon a heedless world I at
least expect to be invited by the maker to pose for a sleek
portrait in *Field and Fen* endorsing his brand of rubber
sausage. "Folks," I'll say, "I've rid and spun around in and

cursed this here now tough old sausage for nigh on to—"
It'll be a labor of love.

The Strangest Trout Spot in My World: Of all the many
weird places I know that harbor trout the Old Springhole
on the Whitefish River in Alger County is the strangest of
all. It is a veritable lake, a quarter-mile long and deep, set
down in the middle of a shallow river and fed winter and
summer from both sides by gushing ice-cold springs that
tumble down out of steep crumbly limestone ledges. Both
banks are crowded to the edges by a jungle of tangled cedars.
It is a devil of a place to get a boat into and nine devils of
a place to fly fish without a boat. There is one little fifty-foot
catwalk of limestone on one side that a good roll-caster might
cast from, provided he were only as tall as a midget. I once
tried it on my knees and, in that prayerful attitude and
doubtless due to divine intervention, was rewarded by taking
a lovely trout.

Bait-fishermen naturally haunt the place, and on a good
day the woods along both banks bristle with their protruding
steel girders, much like the peering artillery of rival troops
lined up for point-blank fire. I once came upon an old peg-
legged local character who had hacked a hole in the jungle
through which he was thrusting his girder, lowering a seven-
inch fish into the inky water.

"Just ketch one?" I said, making low fish talk.

"Naw," he replied. "That's my bait. Can't ya see it's a
chub?"

Lo, it *was* a chub. "Y-you mean you use *that* for bait?" I
gasped incredulously.

"Damn right I do!" he snapped. "Caught a twenty-two-
inch brook yesterday with a helluva bigger chub." He
squinted up at me in my diving suit and endless parapher-

nalia. "And how many like *that* do *you* ketch with them there goddam little house moths?"

I gulped and fought my way on downstream.

In the July or August dog days when the temperatures rise and the water levels go down, all the big trout for miles around seem to congregate in this fabulous trout haven. Some of the most dramatic big-fish rises I have ever seen occur there. (I have never caught an undersized trout there nor seen one come from the place.) Yet the few times I have found the hardihood to tote my rubber boat in there one wouldn't think a trout ever had dwelt there. That's fisherman's luck, of course, but someday I'll hit. . . .

Bears I've Never Met: I've seen dozens of them from cars but I'm delighted to report that never yet have I met one face to face while on foot. Yet I've heard them and smelled them—they smell like an unmanicured pig—and one time I even contrived to get myself caught between a feeding bear and a muddy, unwadable beaver dam. Here's how it happened: Tommy Cole and I had gone up to the Salmon Trout Creek to fish a certain productive beaver dam. Tommy and I rigged up while we watched a sprightly rise. I then left Tommy and crossed on the dam and worked my way upstream through a tangle of brambles and raspberry bushes, intently fishing all the while. I had creeled two trout when at length I heard Tommy crashing through the thick brambles right behind me.

"Come on out here, Tommy," I said. "The going's much better out here." The crashing continued. "Tommy," I called more urgently.

"Woof," Tommy grunted in my ear, and then I heard the greedy slurping of the unseen bear feeding on the raspberries not more than two rod lengths behind me. He had been there all the while. . . .

"*Taw-o-me!*" I wailed like a banshee. The bear fell ominously silent.

"Halloo-oo!" Tommy answered, his voice floating thinly from far downstream, where I later found he'd gone to find a rumored new beaver dam.

"I—I'm a-coming!" I answered, and since I had successfully fished my way into this mess (the bear was doubtless just plain awed by my casting ability), I decided to fish my way out of it, though I'll admit I was glad no one was around making movies of my feverish casts.

This neck of the woods is crammed with black bears and yet I've heard of but two cases of a bear attacking a human —once from hunger (the bear stole a baby out of a forester's crib) and once because a man was molesting the bear's cubs. But I was plenty scared that day. The reason I had the hay up my neck with *this* bear was because I feared that he might think that I was challenging his possession of the raspberry patch. And raspberries were scarce that year. I wasn't, of course, and in fact I haven't ever been able to enjoy this wild fruit since—'though Tommy Cole still gives me the raspberry over the way I came charging pell-mell down creek to join him. He claims that on that day I joined the immortals: that I'm one of the few fishermen in captivity who ever made the 100-yard dash in ten seconds using hip boots for track shoes.

Getting Close to Trout: Wary as trout are, this can be done. It can be done because trout fishermen, including this one, constantly do it. Some fishermen, like Hewitt, get real chummy and even manage to touch them with their hands —"tickling" it's called—but I've never got quite that far, or rather, come that close. All river and stream trout normally lie facing upstream. It is surprising how close one can come to them by approaching from below. But Indian stealth and infinite patience are two absolute requirements.

I have approached solitary feeding trout so close that I could have reached out and touched their feeding circles with my rod tip, and in fact had finally to *retreat* in order to make a presentable cast. The noise of the current, the fact that the fish is facing away, and his concentration on feeding are doubtless all factors making this possible. And if a relatively clumsy fisherman can get this close it is small wonder, then, that the lightning otter can sneak up and grab a trout.

Again, believe it or not, I have on a number of occasions suddenly found myself in the midst of a wild general rise of big feeding trout—maddening rises in which I could not possibly match the hatch—where I was morally certain I would have had a much better chance if I merely reached out and tried to take them with my landing net, I was that close.

The moral of all this, if there is any, is that a man needn't be a whing-ding tournament distance caster to present a decent dry fly. All he needs to do is learn to stalk up close and make an *accurate* short cast before his fish. In the meantime he isn't scaring the bejabbers out of the *other* trout and keeping down *all* the dormant but potential risers that might lie between him and his distant riser. Most rookie fly casters (and too many experienced ones) try to handle way too much line. I raise twice as many fish within thirty feet or less, in my dry-fly work, than I ever do beyond that distance. Forget the histrionics and dramatics and the business of trying to impress your fellows with what a hell of a power-caster you are. It's worth repeating: work up close and make a short accurate cast. If you must show off take up amateur dramatics next winter. That slinky Naomi Goldfinch is simply dying to have you hold her in your big strong arms.

Tying Your Own: Alas, I've tried and I've sighed and all but cried, but I simply can't seem to tie a decent fly. Apparently I fell on my head when I was a baby or something. All my flies come out like old feather dusters. And I really envy those fishermen who can tie a good fly because it seems to me there is a special satisfaction, not to mention a delicate massage to the ego, in luring a trout with one's own creation; something akin to playing a solo part in one's own symphonic composition and watching the glittering ladies out front heaving and sighing and swooning with emotion.

Aside from these intangible values, however, there is a definite practical value in being able to tie up precisely the fly you want. After all, *you* are the only person that really knows what you want—you were there and saw the wondrous sights. There are flies I still dream about that are apparently so filmy and fugitive—or simple—that I cannot seem to impart my dream to any tier I know. Perhaps I merely confess the limitations and poverty of my prose.

There is one big compensation I have observed in *not* being able to tie flies: the few good fishermen-tiers I know seem to spend most of the season manacled to their vises; they consume more time in tying flies than in fishing. And I doubt that many fishermen save any money tying their own; many of them seem promptly to develop an occupational malady that results in a sort of evangelistic fervor, a missionary zeal, to promulgate some particular pattern. Most of the fishermen-tiers I know *give* away most of their flies.

Despite these minor vices of the fly vise, however, I'll take the chance on being manacled and evangelistic and all the rest; I still long to tie a fly that doesn't always contrive to look like a motheaten Fuller brush. Then what a whiz-kid I'd really be on a trout stream!

Leader Sinks: Try lava soap. However dark remains your soul and buoyant your leaders you'll at least keep your hands clean.

Fly Dope: If you are hardy enough, smoke Italian cigars. They smell like a burning peat bog mixed with smoldering Bermuda onions but they're the best damned unlabeled DDT on the market; all mosquitoes in the same township immediately shrivel and zoom to earth. (Fellow fishermen occasionally follow suit.) However, if you are soft and effete, use formula 448. On the other hand one of the most popular fly dopes on the market is the best little varnish remover I've ever seen.

Domestic Relations: Invite your wife to go fishing during the height of fly time. Press her to join you. Tell her the *only* real canker in your fishing is missing her bright presence by your side. Put a quaver in your voice. "It's nice to go fishing with the fellows and all, Honey, but . . ." is a good opening gambit. If successful in luring her give her sweet-ened water for fly dope. This harrowing experience will hold her nicely for a year. If she recoils in horror and refuses to go, still remembering the last time, she can nevertheless cherish the memory of that sweet generous gesture by her man. Either way you lay up red points and emerge as a real good guy. A sly fisherman can get a lot of domestic mileage from an occasional well-placed invitation of this kind.

Preservation of Fly Lines: Drunk or sober, always dry your fly line as soon as possible after leaving the water. In a pinch wind it around your whisky bottle, or else lay it out in loose coils in a shoe box. Even wrap it around yourself if necessary —or else mail it to me. More fishing equipment is ruined through thoughtless neglect than ever it is by use on laughing trout waters.

"You Shoulda Been Here Last Week!": Drill these whimsical characters between the eyes at forty paces.

Out-of-Town Guests Who Invite Themselves: Tell them you've given your fly rods to charity and taken up plug-casting for wormy bass—or else that, hurray, the doctor thinks those ugly spots on Junior may not be smallpox after all.

Out-of-Town Guests You Want to Come: Wire them that an eccentric old Finn west of here just showed you a secret pond where the trout measure three feet between the eyes —but that none of the bumpkins around here can ketch 'em, not even *you.* This challenge will fetch your man running every time.

Women Fishermen: Avoid them. One kind will quietly outfish you and generally get in your hair while another variety will come down with the vapors and want to go home just when the rise gets under way. Avoid all of them like woodticks.

Trout Fishermen: Most people avoid *them* like woodticks. They're regarded in many quarters as tricky and deceitful, subtle and full of guile, and as men who lie just to keep their hands in. But don't blame fishermen: after all they devote their lives to practicing these black arts on the stream, a topsy-turvy world where these vices are hailed as virtues.

144

Be reasonable and reflect that fishermen just can't help acting the same way on the few occasions they mingle in the society of ordinary men. That is why so many normal people regard fishermen as being no damned good. Drat it, men, we're simply misunderstood.

17

The Old and the Proud

I HEARD the rhythmic whine and whish of his fly line before I saw him.

It was late afternoon and I was sitting on the edge of a flood-blasted high gravel bank overlooking a wide bend in the Big Escanaba River, leaning against one of a whispering stand of white pines, sipping a tepid can of beer and waiting for the evening rise. The sun was curving down and half of the river was already in shadow. "*Whish*," sang the music of the unseen fly line, and I leaned forward craning to glimpse the sturdy fisherman who had penetrated to such a remote stretch on one of my favorite trout streams.

Then he rounded the bend below me, wading up over his waist, breasting the deep powerful current, inching along, a tottering old fisherman supporting and pushing himself along with a long-handled landing net which also served as a wading staff. As I sat watching, a good trout rose between us. The old man saw it, too, and paused and braced himself against the current. He then paid out his line—false-casting to dry the fly and at the same time extend his line—and then, when I had about concluded he would never release the thing, whished out and delivered a beautiful curling upstream dry-fly cast. The fish rose and took the fly almost as it landed and I leaned forward watching the old fisherman as he expertly gathered in his slack, like a man harvesting grapes. He then suddenly whipped out his long-handled net and scooped in the fish as it passed him on its downstream run. It was a spanking beauty and I sat chewing my lip with envy.

The old fisherman held up his glistening fish and admired it and then creeled it. He then seemed to spend an interminable time selecting and tying on a new fly. He carried a little magnifying glass through which he peered at his fly boxes like a scientist bending over his retorts. In the meantime two more nice fish had risen between us, a circumstance which would have normally spurred me into action—not there, indeed, for this was now the old man's stretch—but I was held riveted to the spot by the sheer artistry and pluck of the old man's performance. The ritual of choosing and tying on the fly completed, it must have taken him another five or ten minutes to push and maneuver himself against the urgent river to assume his chosen casting position for the lower rising trout. Again there was the expert, careful, painstaking cast; again the obedient take on the first float; and again the sudden deft netting of the fish on its first downstream run. I thought the tottering old gentleman would surely founder and drown as he fought up through even deeper water to try for the third trout. He seemed to teeter in the current, like a wavering tightrope walker, and I restrained an impulse to shout a warning. Even *I*, a relative adolescent, had never dared wade up through this particular deep bend. . . . But the old man didn't drown and he calmly took the trout —again in as impressive a display of quiet fishing artistry as I had ever seen.

Here, I told myself, was a *real* fly fisherman, cool, deliberate, cagey, who for all the disabilities of his years could plainly fish rings around me and all the rest of my eager fishing pals. His performance was an illustrated lecture on one of the hardest of fundamentals for fishermen to learn: *easy does it.* But my heart went out to him as he continued to struggle manfully against the insistent current to reach still a new rise opposite and a little above me. On he came, like a man shackled by nightmare, still using his landing net as a staff. When he had fought his way opposite me I couldn't resist offering my nickel's worth of comment.

"Nice job of fishin'," I said, with all the foolhardy aplomb of the winner of a local dance marathon undertaking to compliment Nijinsky.

He glanced quickly up at me—one keen, appraising, wrinkled glance—and then away, as though I were a squirrel scolding and chattering on a bough. "Hm," he sniffed, that was all; just "Hm."

"Wouldn't it be a lot easier," I said, still filled with concern and still determined to take the fatal plunge, "wouldn't it be a lot easier if you fished downstream?"

The effect of this remark was as though I had deliberately impaled the old man with my fly or thrown a rock at his rising trout. His whole body seemed to shudder and recoil; then he stood stock-still and sighted me through his glasses, adjusting them, as though at last discovering that I was not a foolish squirrel but rather some new species of buzzing and pestiferous insect. "Harrumph," he snorted. "Listen, young fella," he said, "I'd sooner sit on my prat on the public dock at Lake Michigamme and plunk night crawlers for bass than *ever* fish a wet fly!"

Thus shriveled, I sat there red-faced and watched him teeter and struggle out of sight around the bend above. On the way he paused and took two more lovely trout.

This exchange of pleasantries between trout fishermen took place some fifteen years ago. Since then my anonymous old dry-fly purist has doubtless been gathered into the place where the meadows are always green and the trout always rising; but the lesson of our brief meeting was well learned. Ever since then my fellow fishermen may have at their trout from balloons or diving bells, for my part, without dredging up a single comment from me. And while I still fish the ignominious wet fly just as avidly as the lowly plunkers plunk for bass at Lake Michigamme, I have since learned that when dry-fly fishing is in season (alas, it frequently isn't in our chilly and temperamental northern waters) it is the most thrilling and rewarding—and exacting—of all methods of taking the fighting trout.

Whenever the day is dying and I find myself sitting on that particular high water-gouged bank on the Big Escanaba waiting for the evening rise, the brave words of that gallant old fisherman keep echoing and ringing in my ears—and lending them color, too. "Listen, young fella, I'd sooner sit on my prat on the public dock at Lake Michigamme and plunk night crawlers for bass than *ever* fish a wet fly!"

I have never forgotten this testy proud old man. In my mind's eye I can see him now. It is a still evening and he is breasting the deep celestial waters that run through green pastures. He is inching along with his glistening rod and his staff. A heavenly trout rises. He pauses and prepares to make one of his cool deliberate casts. His magic wand flashes and bends. "Whish," sings the line—"Whish," it goes, ever *"Whish."* . . .

18

Straight Up at Dinty's

A GOOD many people seem constitutionally unable to give proper directions. All want to; many yearn to; but, alas, few can correctly tell the way. The matter seems to have little or no connection with their intelligence or virtue; they simply can't coherently describe where they've been or how they got there.

Take the time last fall Jim Clancey and I were proceeding to Covington in the old fish car to hunt partridge. Trying to find a short cut we instead found ourselves snarled in a maze of windfallen and partridgy old logging roads. Away the birds flew, "Bang, *bang!*" our cannons blew. . . . We finally hewed and bombarded our way to the grand intersection of a dozen-odd roads flying off in all directions, all of them bad. At the very hub of this maze stood an old Finn sharpening an ax.

Jim leered out the car window. "My good man," he began suavely, and for a moment I thought he was going to recite "Woodman-spare-that-tree." "My good man," he repeated, "which of these roads can we take to Covington?"

The old Finn leered back, reflected and shrugged, then spat and spoke. "Any of dem, dat's all right, I doan care," he said, turning sadly away. Like ourselves, magnanimity could go no further. . . .

Yes, I have ruefully learned that many if not most people cannot properly direct their needy fellows, say, to an illuminated outhouse forty paces away. Especially is this true of woods directions. They might possibly remember that you should turn right at Macy's corner but not at that storm-blasted pine. They have simply never observed the storm-blasted pine. But they themselves can invariably find the place you seek, depending upon a vague and woolly sort of mental Braille, much as many people manage to remember phone numbers by a convoluted process of association that would shame Rube Goldberg.

Often have I been "directed" to secret trout streams in deep valleys and instead wound up on bald granite bluffs. At least in that way I saved lots of my favorite flies—and there was always the view. . . . Beware, too, of home-grown hand-loomed maps; they serve only to engrave the error and compound the confusion. Some hapless hunters and fishermen who have followed such maps have sprouted beards as long as those of gay Chamber of Commerce centennial celebrants before they were rescued and led away to the barber. Perhaps the biggest weakness in giving woods directions is the careful failure of the average director or cartographer to indicate (a) important turn-offs and (b) the roads or trails one *shouldn't* take. There was the day last spring that an amiable bartender undertook to direct me to Blair Pond in adjoining Baraga County. His fuzzy counsel was so typical it should have been preserved on tape.

"Blair Pond, hey? That's easy. Hm. . . . First you drive to the town of L'Anse," my guide began boldly.

"We now find ourselves in the sleepy logging village of L'Anse," I intoned in the soothing voice of the travelogue movies.

"Then you take and drive out just past that gas station and sorta turn off . . ." He paused and blinked. Ah, we were in trouble already.

Surprised: "Oh, so L'Anse has a *gas* station now? My, my . . . time marches on. . . . When in the world did they ever get *that?*"

Pouting: "You turn off at the Standard Oil station, dammit!"

Reflecting: "Hm. . . . Offhand I recall at least *three* Standard stations in the sleepy logging village of L'Anse."

Doggedly: "It's the one across from the Shell station."

"And pray tell where in hell is the Shell station?"

Triumphant: "Just across from the Standard station."

The man had me there. Indubitably. There was a long pause. Perhaps, I thought, it would be better if we started from scratch. Brightly, offhandedly: "Say, chum, could you tell me the way to Blair Pond?"

Rapidly: "You go to L'Anse and turn off at the Standard station."

"Hm. We two seem to have been there before. Did you ever, perchance, pump gas before you were promoted to pumping beer? No? Well anyway, do you sorta turn off to the left or to the right?"

"Neither. Sorta slantwise like . . ." He waved his hands vaguely, like an ultra-modern sculptor fashioning a buttock.

"Kind of a slow curve, see? Then you go two-three miles and you come to a farm with a white horse grazing in the pasture—"

Interrupting: "But suppose the white horse isn't hungry? Suppose he's out working? Or off running in the Derby? Or hanging around a New York advertising agency waiting to pose for a whisky ad? Or has dyed himself? Or has himself died? Or—?"

Grimly: "Look, fella, you want to know where this here place is at or don't you? I'm tryin' to do you a favor."

Softly: "I'm dying to."

Leaving the white horse at the turn: "You don't turn off where the white horse is grazing but keep going straight. A mile or two past there—or is it three?—you'll come to a place where a nice-looking Finnish girl is selling blueberries under a tree." He waved his hands some more and continued wistfully. "Yep, a fine-looking Finnish girl. . . . Then you sorta turn off just past her on a two-rut road and drive straight in to the pond. You can't miss it!"

"This Finnish girl—does she always sell her blueberries in May? Oh, I get it—they're preserved in Mason fruit jars. Tell me, must one leave a deposit on the jar? Does she do her stuff right under the tree? And what kind of a tree—?"

But my cowardly bartender was retreating to the back room, running, hurling his last words over his shoulder. "Gotta tap a new keg— Don't ketch 'em all. . . . Good luck. . . . So long, pal."

Naturally I never did find the fabled white horse or the Blueberry Girl, let alone Blair Pond. But I did miraculously avoid any bald granite bluffs. Instead I stumbled into a virgin beaver dam loaded with brook trout. Wanna find the place? It's dead easy, friend. Just take and go to L'Anse and sorta turn off like when you see that big dumpling cumulus cloud. Park the car kinda off to the side of the cloud to avoid rain. The damn dam lies straight ahead. You can't possibly miss it!

19

The Old Fox

It was about noon when I pulled out of the stream at the ruins of the old logging dam and fought my way to the top of the shattered old dam through the inevitable tangle of alders. There I sat and drank in the view, looking far up and down the sparkling and dancing Yellow Dog River, enjoying the comparatively cool breeze, and waiting for Carroll to join me for our noonday sandwich. I could still see evidences of the old dam lying jumbled all about me: great square rusty hand-forged spikes still protruding from the rotting timbers. I reflected that the nearly forgotten white pine lumberjacks were giants in their day, while today's so-called "lumberjacks" are merely unhappy mosquito-bitten mechanics caught far away from home. . . .

The remote Yellow Dog River is a fabulous little rocking-chair stream; as willful and turbulent and wenchy as a handsome native dancer; the kind of seductive trout stream that keeps fishermen misty-eyed and mumbling to themselves trying to fathom its tempestuous moods and to realize its promise. But few are the fishermen that ever solve or subdue it. Its virtually unending series of shallow pockets and pools, gravelly riffles and rapids, wild chutes and quiet glides offer a bewildering variety of fishing and harbor some of the loveliest trout in Michigan. The *only* problem is to get on to them.

This particular day Carroll and I had been slugging away at the problem since shortly after sunup. I still didn't know how he was doing, but I ruefully knew that I, at least, was still several thousand light years away from the solution. Fishing mostly downstream I had caught or pricked scores of dancy, spittin' little trout. Out of desperation and low pride I had finally kept several seven- and eight-inchers for the fry pan (we had planned our usual stream-side trout fry to augment our sandwiches). But I hadn't so much as seen a decent rising trout much less raised one to the fly. Mostly I had fished downstream wet or occasionally slack-line dry because of the difficulty of making a decently controlled upstream cast in the brushy, unkempt little stream. I was getting a trifle despondent and anxious for Carroll to join me so that I could lay the sly preliminary groundwork for a move on to other more fishable if less fabulous trout waters. And I needed his vote.

But where was Carroll? I looked at my big silver watch, the kind that strikes the hour and the quarter hours, and saw that it was past twelve-thirty. A couple of partridge in the woods back of me suddenly decided to get into the time act, so they began beating their tom-toms, beginning in their slow deliberate rhythmic locomotive fashion, like a college cheer, and concluding in a rapid ecstatic ascending crescendo of fluttering wings. Out of boredom more than hunger

I fished out my sandwich and ate it; then I filled and tamped and lit my pipe and just sat there looking down the glittering serpentine course of the river waiting for tardy Carroll to join me. When Old Big Ben struck one I knocked out my pipe and ground out the embers and moved slowly down river along the heavily wooded bank in quest of the missing fisherman.

One-fifteen chimed; then one-thirty; then I began to get a little worried. Where was my man? Carroll was usually prompt in meeting at the agreed time and place. And this was pretty wild and woolly country. I got back away from the insistent noise of the stream on a little rise of ground so that I might better both see or hear him if he was in trouble. Still no Carroll. Big Ben tinkled one-forty-five and I was just about to vent one of my bloodcurdling shouts when through a thin grove of dappled poplars I saw a man plodding slowly up the river. I craned to look. Yes, it was Carroll all right; the Old Fox himself. But what was he doing? I peered more closely. Of all things, he was fighting a fish, and a good one, too, judging from the bow in his rod. Feeling like a wallflower at a prom I shook my head in envy and admiration as I watched him creel this handsome specimen. He always carries an old-fashioned rigid wicker creel about the size of a pack basket so there was no way to judge whether this was his sole catch of the day.

I was just about to shout a greeting and try to lure him elsewhere when I saw him tie on another fly and continue fishing. Hm . . . fishing must be fairly good. But where were the long whistling dry-fly casts for which he was locally famous? I quietly moved closer to the river. The old fox was intent as a real fox, stalking, squinting, inching—and delicately casting out *not more than fifteen feet of line!* As I watched him he rose and got on to a respectable trout—a

ten-eleven incher, at least—and released it before my in-
credulous eyes. Then I saw him change flies again and
stealthily inch a few more feet upstream. He paused below
a modest riffle and, still working the short line, rose and was
fast to a lovely trout on his first cast. He postured and turned
like a marionette during the whirling fight. His net sagged
under this specimen, and I stood there entranced while he
fumbled in his creel, as though counting, and then unhooked
and *released* this spanking fish! He then lit a cigarette and
suddenly quit the stream—almost walking into me stealthily
spying on him.

"Ah, good morning, Mister Bear," he said drily.

"You old fox," I said accusingly. "You sly, deceitful, rum-
soaked, double-dealing—er—foxy old fox—what have you been
up to now? I *saw* you release those fish. Have you finally
completely blown your top?"

"Spying on me, were you?" Carroll grew mock-indignant.
"Creeping up on me unbeknownst and ferreting out my
trade secrets, were you? Well, if you *must* know I threw
the first one back because he was too small—I've already put
back many bigger ones—and the last one because I discovered I already had my limit. I had merely lost count. But
how'd you do, Izaak Walton, Junior?"

I swallowed hard and ignored this barb. "Lemme see
'em," I demanded.

"Sure, sure," Carroll answered loftily. "The proof of the
pudding gathers no moss." He hefted his heavy pack basket
off his shoulder and *poured* out a torrent of big trout upon
the ferns—perhaps the loveliest catch I have ever seen, at
least outside of Canada.

I sank to my knees in an unfamiliar attitude of prayer and
stared at them in awe. Fifteen glistening trout they were—
mixed browns, rainbows, and brooks—and all of them two-

dollar fish, that is, fifteen inches or over. I shook my head. "My heavenly days," I murmured, a defeated and broken man, corroded with envy.

"How'd you do?" Carroll repeated sweetly, plunging the needle farther.

Reaching in my sweat-dampened pocket I fished out my answer—two wrinkled dollar bills—and bleakly handed them to him. "Kept four dwarfed grandchildren of your smallest fish," I said. "But how did you *do* it?" I went on, incredulously. "What'd you *use*, man—Parisian postcards?"

"Oh, I used only one fly," Carroll answered, stifling a yawn, as offensively modest as a man who'd just swum the Channel with one arm tied behind his back—and then refused to be photographed.

"You lying fox—I just *saw* you change flies twice."

"Don't be hasty, chum—I only used one fly pattern—but I put on a fresh fly after every fish. Today they were temperance trout—they wanted them strictly dry. I kept nothing under fifteen inches. Boy oh boy, what a day, what a stream."

"But what fly was it?" I demanded. *"Confess,* damn it!"

Carroll shrugged and widened his hands and bowed his head in mock surrender. "You've caught me, pal—it was the little Betty McNault—number 16."

Between them those two old foxes Tommy Cole and Carroll Rushton have perhaps taught me most of what I was ever able to absorb about the mysteries of fly fishing for trout. Carroll it was that initiated me into the roll cast, perhaps the only department of the sport in which I might excel him. Both he and Tommy are slow, deliberate, undramatic fishermen, almost sleepily casual performers, true disciples of the all-important *easy does it*. More than being excellent fishermen they are philosophers who fish. Both have fly-fished for many years and both are battle-scarred old foxes of the stream who possess to an astonishing degree that diabolical "fish sense" coupled with fishing dexterity that I have mentioned earlier. (Young Henry Scarffe, with whom I am currently "going steady"—as my wife calls my fishing romances—is another such comer.) And so it was that on that enchanted day on the Yellow Dog I learned once and for all the invaluable lesson of the short accurate dry-fly upstream cast. I've never forgotten it.

"Nobody but a magician can manage an accurate long cast in these brambles," Carroll finally relented and explained between mouthfuls of sandwich. "All you can accomplish is to put the fish down in those very intervening places where you might otherwise have a Chinaman's chance to take them—the ones lying there right before your patrician and alcoholic nose. So what do you do? You get disgusted and stubborn and careless and try to fish downstream and, in these clear waters, only manage to scare the pants off of every decent trout within fifty feet. You've thoughtfully been herding the big ones down to me all morning. And all you get are the Junior Leaguers. But don't you see— in these noisy tumbling waters from *below* you can almost walk up and pet these fish. Do you follow me, my disconsolate friend?"

"Yes, sir," I answered meekly.

"Therefore," he went on, "if you would only muster the wit and the patience to try, you will find that you can float a dainty cast directly over their suspected lies. And you don't miss nearly so many fish as on the imperceptibly delayed strike involved in long upstream casts on these fast shallow waters." Carroll paused. "But enough of this pompous lecturing. Class is dismissed. . . . Get going, now, while I clean out these fish. Here, take a half-dozen of these virgin Betties."

I took the flies humbly and followed instructions—and in little over a half-hour had taken six trout between ten and fifteen inches. I had also raised several more, one a spaniel. They were really on the prod that day, though needless to say the Yellow Dog doesn't always deliver that way. But it is a rare day when Carroll Rushton doesn't dredge up a companion old fox to enable him to relieve me of one or two of those officially engraved likenesses of George Washington so thoughtfully provided by the U. S. Mint.

As for the Betty McNault (I have seen it also variously spelled McNall and McNoll), it is a dainty little hackled hair fly, tied and appearing much like a minor variant of that old reliable, the Royal Coachman. It is a tremendously versatile fly; one that can be fished either wet or dry. Oddly enough, like so many effective flies it looks like no natural fly I've ever seen floating on a stream. Carroll always carries oodles of them, in all smaller sizes, but the number 16 is far and away his favorite—especially, as I wryly discovered, for stalking big trout upstream in the tumbling and fumbling Yellow Dog.

The only thing Carroll hasn't been able to impart to me, unfortunately, is perhaps the most important thing. It is this: how in the bloomin' blazes does he *know* where the favorite lies of the big trout are? Ah, there's the rub! That, alas, is one of the fascinating mysteries of fishing; here is an instinct, a secret sense, that no fisherman can ever divulge to another—even if he would. And so, to this day, I continue to pay him tribute regularly in damp one- and two-dollar installments. (I hope my wife never reads this.) But I have grown philosophical about it all—I now regard it as money well spent, a payment more in the nature of a deserved tuition, so to speak, to be able to study at the casting elbow of the Old Fox himself.

20

The Voyage

LOUIE BONETTI sidled up to my law office one beautiful August morning, bowing and scraping and grinning, hat in hand—"Gooda mornin', Mister Yon"—and slipped into the chair opposite me. For some obscure reason the dusty shelves of systematically unread law books and the various diplomas and certificates and somber pictures of notaries, dead fish, and politicians that adorned my walls seemed always unduly to impress Louie, because these were the only occasions I ever saw him remove his hat for anyone or anything—although you will remember, he did *tip* his hat when he said, "Gooda mornin', Mister Bear!"

"Luke, Yon," he said, grinning and puffing away at his gnarled Italian cigar. "Luke, I jes' talka some people over my a place, an' dey tella me confidench where dey catcha one hell of a beeg mess a brooka trout las' night."

"You *mean* it, Louie?" I said, suddenly sitting up all alert.

Louie's "place" was his tavern, of course, run by his two strapping sons, Geno and Guido. I had learned that Louie heard many strange and wonderful tales from his arid customers—and also delivered himself of quite a few. "Do you mean it, Louie?" I repeated.

"Sure, sure t'ing—dese people gooda people, dey sometime tella da trut'." Louie shrugged and threw up both hands, palms up. "An' he's a nice a day an' you my gooda fran an' I t'ink maybe I take a you dere dis aft. W'at you t'ink?"

Louie had chosen and cast his lure well. "Do we need a boat, Louie?" I said, already mentally canceling appointments and rearranging my modest affairs.

"Ya, ya," Louie answered. "We gotta have da boat. He's a kinda bad a place. Dis here a spot he's a west of here on swampy stretch of Meedle Escanaba. Leedle feeder crick he come right in where da beeg a trout he hang aroun'. Dat's da dope."

"Can we make it in one afternoon, Louie?"

"Sure, sure," Louie reassured me. "Easy. . . . Udder people—gooda people—tella me confidench a shorta cut dat even dese people who tella me da place doan know."

It was all a little complicated, but by then my nostrils were flaring and my eyes were wide and awash with stardust. "When and where do we meet?" I said, as Louie moved to the door, hat still in hand.

"Hm. . . . Picka me up behind da place at twelva-t'irt—an' be sure you bring a da leedle boat."

"O.K., Louie," I said, and thus the great voyage was planned.

At 1:30 Louie and I rattled over the loose planking of the logging bridge of the Middle Escanaba in search of Louie's short cut. I stopped the fish car on the other side and grew thoughtful. "Look, Louie," I said, "why don't we just put the boat in here and paddle up to the new hot spot?"

"*Non, non,*" Louie answered, "Too far. An' maybe udder people dey see us on way an den dey fine our new a spot. Anyway, lak I tella you, I know da swella shorta cut. *Drive on!*"

Commander Bonetti had taken over, and few were the men who could resist his peculiar brand of hypnosis. He should have been a conjurer or a trial lawyer; he was a natural specialist in persuading the complete abdication of reason.

"Stoppa da car!" Louie ordered, after we had proceeded north on the dusty road nearly five miles. "Dis here da shorta cut." I slammed on the brakes and we were overtaken by our own dust storm.

We had stopped at a little tag-alder creek about four feet wide that girdled and squeezed itself to run under the dirt road through an iron pipe. Louie had already leapt out and was untying the cedar boat from the trailer.

I shook my head. "Looks pretty small to me for boating," I said, dubiously stroking my chin.

"*Non, non,* Yon." He widened his arms. "He gets a beeg beeg down jes' a leedle way. Anyway, he's a gooda shorta cut."

"Just how far down is it to this hot spot on the main river, Louie?" I asked.

"Hm . . . maybe two-t'ree 'ondred yard, maybe less," Louie answered airily. "Anyway, he's swella shorta cut."

I scratched the top of my head and squinted one eye. "Look, Louie," I said, "how in hell can the big river be only a few hundred yards away when we crossed the damned thing five miles *south* of here?"

Louie sighed over my obtuseness and crouched in the

middle of the sandy road and drew a map with his finger. He had now adopted the title of master cartographer of the expedition. "Luke, Yon," he lectured patiently, wagging his dusty map finger at me. "Da beeg riv' he runna easta-west across da breedge, yes, jes' lak a dis, see?"

"I see," I answered meekly, appropriately chastened.

"Den da riv' maka beeg a loop nort' up a dis a way, lak a dis, see?"—Louie the mapmaker described a big loop north—"an' almos' hita da road right here, see?"

"Yes."

"Den dis here a crick he runna two-t'ree 'ondred yard down dis a way, see?"

"Yes."

"Den we hita da hotta spot an feesh—an' den we feesh an' float an' float an' feesh all da way down da riv' to da breedge, see?"

"Yes," I answered. "But after we get down to the wooden bridge how'n hell do we get way back up *here* to get the car and trailer?" I thought I really had him there.

But Louie was equal to anything. "Hm . . . da lucky a man what get da beegest feesh—he sit on breedge an' watcha da feesh an' drinka da whisk'. *He doan walk.*"

"O.K., Louie," I said, accepting his challenge. We tossed off the boat and threw in our gear and prepared to shove off. Just as an afterthought I threw in an ax.

Commander Bonetti sat straight as an arrow in the bow of the nine-foot cedar boat, like his "Christa Columb." "Alla set, Yon?" he said, impatient to get at his big secret trout lying there in wait such a few feet away.

"All set, Louie," I said, shoving on the culvert with my paddle. The historic voyage was away. I glanced at my watch. It was 1:55.

I cannot truthfully say that I have ever seen a river that ran uphill but I can say that I saw one creek that got smaller and smaller the farther down it one got. We were on it that day. By the time we had pushed and shoved and hacked our way downstream a hundred yards it was hideously plain that there was no turning back; even *Louie* couldn't have managed that.

"Kinda brushy, Louie," I said softly, avoiding his eyes and tossing a bushel or so of tag-alder branches out of the boat.

"On'y leedle farder," Louie grunted, leaping out of the boat in his hip boots and *pulling* the boat and me down through the next jungle of tag alders that loomed ahead. I leaned back like Cleopatra floating on the Nile.

I could go on and on, tracing each tortuous *mile* of that fantastic voyage; telling about the scores of times we had to stop and chop a path to get the boat through the horrible tangle, lift it over logs and endless tiny beaver dams, and of the scores of times we had to empty the boat of heaps of twigs and rotten branches. We were doubtless the only men in history, white or red, drunk or sober, who had ever been foolish enough to pull a boat down that particular creek. Rogers' Rangers had had a basket picnic.

"On'y leedle farder," Louie chanted each time we ran into a particularly discouraging new wall of obstruction. It was no longer a question of fishing; all that was long since sweated out of us. It had become a grim question of getting ourselves out of there and saving the boat.

At 9:58 that night—eight hours later—we gained the river, and while we couldn't even see each other any longer we could hear the big feeding trout flopping all around us.

By 10:17 we had negotiated the short easy float down to the wooden bridge! On the way wily Louie had surreptitiously run out his girder and caught himself an eight-inch trout. By midnight I had walked up to and returned with the fish car and trailer; and by 1:58 Louie and I were arm and arm in the back booth of his "place," sweat-stained and grimy, alder twigs coming out of our ears, and both drunker than skunks on but two rounds of bar whisky. The fishermen were home from the bog. . . .

The next morning grinning Louie sidled up to the office, hat in hand. "Yon," he announced, "da people my place jes' tella me 'bout gooda trout a place."

I groaned and recoiled arthritically in my chair. "Any short cuts, Louie?" I demanded.

"No shorta cuts," Louie answered, the grin spreading.

"You swear?" I pressed him.

"Hones' crossa my heart, Yon," Louie answered, doing it.

I leaned back with a sigh. "Tell me about it, Louie—and can I *fly* fish there?"

"You can fly lak ever't'ing," Louie answered, still grinning and crossing his heart once more.

During my addled career as a trout fisherman I have gone on a lot of wild-goose chases, and I ruefully expect to go on a lot more before I hang up my waders. Only a fraction of these mad expeditions are confessed in this book, but you have now heard about the wild-goose chase that, in my considerable wry experience in chasing geese, I consider the goose chase to end all goose chases. I do not expect or want ever to equal or surpass it unless, perchance, one day I take off in search of the restless spirit of Louie or the moon.

Finally, I do not wish disloyally to leave the impression that A. Louis Bonetti was not a good woodsman. He was, in fact, one of the best I've ever known; one of those rare individuals who disdain compasses and such truck, who never forget a road or a trail or a marker, who always *know* where they are. He was a natural primitive. The main thing wrong with Louie was that he was gullible; he *listened* to other people; and the main thing wrong with me was that I am gullible; and I listened to Louie when he had been listening to other people. If Louie had once *been* to a place himself, he could remember every physical detail twenty years later, and no mistake; but when he listened to other people and I listened to Louie—together we made a soaring championship team of wild-goose chasers that could have taken on the world.

And you, Louie, wherever you are and whatever you may be doing—all is forgiven. I wouldn't have missed a single moment of our great voyage together. And may you have an unobstructed downstream float to paradise by the shortest cut of all.

21

The Last Day

EACH year it is the same: this time, we tell ourselves, the doze and stitch and murmur of summer can never end; this season time will surely stand still in its tracks. Yet the hazy and glorious days glide by on golden wings, and presently here and there the leaves grow tinted by subtle fairy paintbrushes and flash their red warnings of impending fall. Even the trout become more brilliant in hue and grow heavy and loaded with spawn. And then, lo, one day we tired fishermen drag ourselves abroad only to discover that the stricken summer has waned into colorful northern autumn, like a beautiful woman flushed with the fevers of approaching death. It is the last day of fishing; the annual hibernation is once again at hand.

To this fisherman, at least, with all of its sadness and nostalgia the end of fishing is not unmixed with a sense of relief and release. No more is one oppressed by the curious compulsion of the chase; no more the driving sense of urgency that fills the eyes of fishermen with flecks of stardust shot through with mad gleams of lunacy. Reason is temporarily restored. The precious rods can now be leisurely gone over and stashed; the lines cleaned and stored; the boots hung up by their feet, and all the rest of the sad ritual. Yes, and with a little luck perhaps diplomatic relations can even be restored with those strange but vaguely familiar ladies with whom we have been oh so absently sharing our bedrooms all summer long.

For many years I have speculated on the precise nature of the drives that possess a presumably reasonable man and turn him into that quietly mad creature we call a fisherman. I am satisfied that it is not merely the urge to kill and possess. In fact I now think—like Messrs. Gilbert and Sullivan—that this has nothing to do with the thing, tra la, has nothing to do with the thing. Most fishermen I know are poor or indifferent hunters; as a class they are apt to be a gentle, tweedy, and chicken-hearted lot; and, let us admit it, they are frequently reflective and poky to the point of coma. But allowing for all this I sometimes wonder whether they are not a more atavistic and elemental crew than most of their fellow men—even more so than their bombarding second cousins, the hunters.

All hunters, unless they have got themselves too loaded with cookin' whisky, invariably first *see* their quarry and know precisely what it is, and then deliberately sight and hurl a projectile at it—bullet, arrow, rock or what you will— while the fisherman rarely "sees" his fish in this sense, but rather must expend endless ingenuity and patience in approaching and luring his game to its fate. And perhaps most important, when he is successful he is in actual, pulsing, manual contact with his quarry through the extension of his hand that he calls his line. The real combat only *begins* when he "shoots" his game, that is, sinks the barb. This, to me, marks fishing as at once a more subtle and yet basically more primitive pursuit than hunting, or selling cars or TV sets on time—or even excelling in the absorbing mysteries of corporate financing.

At this late hour I don't want to go in over my waders and poach on the preserves of the psychiatrists. Thank heaven I have never been encouched and so am not qualified to. But sometimes I wonder whether the wild urge to pursue and lure a fighting fish isn't connected somehow with the— er—sexual urges of the fisherman himself. My, my, I've up and said it! Many frustrated and neglected wives of fishermen will doubtless rise up at this point and shout hoarsely, "*What* sexual urges?" Hm, let us see, let us see. . . .

Under the beneficent glow of our present pale tribal customs courtship and marriage can get to be, so my runners inform me, a pretty drab and routine affair; and I divine as though in a dream that some men there are among us who doubtless rebel at constantly laying siege to an already conquered citadel; and unless they are going in for collecting blondes of assorted shades and varying degrees of moral rectitude, fishing and all that goes with it may be the one pursuit that permits them to vent their atavistic impulses and still preserve the tatters of their self-respect. I do not labor the point, but smile evilly and cast my lure lightly upon the troubled waters—and quietly rejoin the drabber subject of the Last Day, the sad refrain upon which I seem to have opened this swan song.

On the last day all fishermen are akin to pallbearers; worse yet, they are pallbearers at their own funerals. Going out on the last day is a job that has to be done, like burying the dead; but their hearts aren't in the enterprise and the day is apt to be ruined by a future that looms ahead as bleak and hopeless as the grave. They may comfort themselves for the ordeal and brace themselves for the purgatory of waiting by telling themselves that it is all for the best. The fisherman's last-day funeral litany is a foggily beautiful and self-deceiving thing and runs something like this: the fishing is no longer sporting; the fisherman himself is dog-tired; the rise can no longer be depended on; the spawn-laden trout are far too easy to catch; and to take them now is to bite off one's nose. Amen.

Yes, on the last day we fishermen can try as we may to incant ourselves into hilarity and acceptance, but our hearts are chilled and our minds are numb. For what we fishermen really want is to go on fishing, fishing, fishing—yes, fishing forever into the great far blue beyond. . . . All that sustains us in our annual autumnal sorrow is the wry knowledge that spring is but two seasons removed. After all, we can sadly croak, it's *only* eight more months till the magic *First Day*!